MW00960445

Chapter One

Blue tumbled and flipped down the staircase, her head narrowly missing a sharp corner, until she finally made contact with the hard concrete floor of the basement. Despite the heavy thud that resonated throughout the space, her witchy powers meant that nothing was broken—not a single bone in her body, or the delicate items that lined the shelves along the walls.

Tiffany, Blue's large black cat familiar, sat at the top of the staircase with her tail twitching and her yellow eyes gleaming. She watched as Blue descended and said, "Can we, like, go to the mall?" Her expression was a mix of curiosity and anticipation.

"Tiffany, I just fell down the stairs."

"Yeah, I know. You should be more careful. You could hurt yourself or something."

Blue huffed and pushed herself up to her elbows, eyes flashing with anger. "You're supposed to be looking out for me," she said, her voice a cross between a growl and a shout. "You don't just sneak up on a person like that."

"I have no idea what you're talking about, Blue. I was just asking if we can go to the mall. I don't know how you managed to throw yourself down the basement steps."

"You startled me, and I tripped."

Tiffany stood over Blue, her eyes wide in mock worry. She let out a long sigh as she repeated her question, "Can we go to the mall?" Her voice was soft and full of fake concern as she flicked her tail back and forth faster.

"We've been over this, Tiff. The mall isn't what it used to be. People don't go there and hang out anymore… or even shop. It's not what you think."

"I'm meeting Brenda." Tiffany stood up and turned around.

Blue sighed. "Brenda is a character from a television show."

"She's my best friend!" Tiffany shrieked.

"She's a character from a show that hasn't been on for over twenty years, Tiffany. Brenda is not your best friend, and we're not going to the mall."

"You're the worst."

"That's up for debate."

Blue groaned as she heaved herself up from the cold, hard steps. Her pants were covered in a light dusting of dirt and cobwebs, but no scrapes or bruises. She moved slowly, clinging to the rough wooden railing as she made her way up the stairs. She had to get going to the shop, so hopefully, she could avoid any further mishaps.

Blue had just settled into the kitchen to make a quick bite for breakfast when a loud thump shook the ceiling above her head. She knew immediately that it was Pepper, her teenage sister who had a tendency to stay up late and sleep in. She glanced at the clock and sighed... Northeast High School began in ten minutes, and unless they left right away, there was no way her sister would make it on time. Blue grabbed her keys and hollered to Pepper that it was time to go.

Blue sighed. She resigned herself to opening the shop a few minutes late. "Come on, Pepper. We need to leave right now," she called up the stairs again.

Pepper's feet thudded against the stairs like a drum roll as she ran down, excitement mixed with anticipation in her wake. At the bottom of the steps, she skidded around the corner into the entryway and stopped short when she saw her older sister. "You're really gonna give me a ride?" she asked, eyes wide with hope.

Blue glanced down at her sister's feet, which were nestled in a pair of chunky royal blue platform Mary Janes. The shoes had thick soles and a three-inch heel, making it unlikely that she'd be able to move quickly. "Well, it's not like you're planning on running there," Blue said, nodding her head towards the shoes.

"Let me grab my bag," Pepper chirped happily.

Blue watched her sister's fingers snake around the straps of her school bag and hoist it from the back of a dining room chair. "You could have just asked for a ride," Blue said, as she noticed the lack of breakfast dishes in the sink. "You know I would have taken you if you'd told me last night. Did you have breakfast?" But Blue already knew the answer to that question. Pepper didn't have any food

3

stashed in her room, and she hadn't made an appearance in the kitchen that morning.

"If I'd asked you last night, you'd have given me the same rehearsed spiel about responsibility and then woke me at the butt crack of dawn anyway." Pepper sighed in frustration and rolled her eyes.

"So, you deliberately ran late so I'd have to take you?" Blue crossed her arms over her chest and started tapping her foot, then stopped abruptly when she realized she was imitating her mother's mannerisms. She quickly uncrossed her arms and waited for an answer.

"I didn't have breakfast." Pepper avoided her question. "Can we hit the Mickey D's drive through?"

"You have six minutes to get to school." Blue hurried into the kitchen and grabbed the Eggos she'd made for herself. She hadn't slathered them in syrup yet, so Pepper could wolf the dry waffles down in the car on the way. At least they had some butter on them.

Blue handed the paper plate with the waffles to Pepper, and they rushed out to the car. "There's no sausage because I was interrupted by my sister being late for school."

Pepper was a bit pouty about the Mickey D's thing, but Blue ignored her. Blue was the one who'd had to give up her breakfast, after all.

Tiffany perched on the window seat and watched as the car slowly backed out of the driveway with Blue and Pepper inside. She looked a bit pouty too.

The school parking lot was a ghost town and the drop-off line was empty. Pepper scrambled out of the car, leaving behind a crumpled paper plate with half a waffle, and sprinted across the pavement. The bell echoed through the air, signaling the beginning of the school day, and she skidded into the building just as the doors closed.

As Blue drove to the candy shop, she finished the last crumbs of a waffle and popped open a lukewarm bottle of Diet Coke. The car had been sitting in the cold all night, so the soda wasn't too bad. Still, she wished she'd brought something better to drink.

Blue pulled her car into the far end of the parking area in front of the candy shop. Although there were still a few spaces closer to the entrance, she kept away from them, leaving them open for customers. The candy shop was rarely busy enough to fill all the spots, but Blue enjoyed the small gesture of hospitality even if no one ever noticed it.

Sucre Bleu sat on one corner of the town square, cattycorner and down the block from the large brick town hall and courthouse. The green park in the center was sprinkled with children playing tag and pigeons cooing from atop a nearby gazebo. The rest of the square was lined with quaint storefronts, each one distinct in their own right. An old bookshop with gleaming bright blue shutters was one of Blue's favorite buildings.

The courthouse loomed impressively over Hemlock Hollow, the old brick exterior frosted with a graceful white dome that glinted in the sunlight. The building was well-preserved, defying its one hundred fifty plus years of age, and the landscaping around it was a masterpiece of manicured perfection. Inside the courthouse, the lobby was abuzz with activity as people paid fines, filed papers, and attended hearings. Courtrooms lined one side of the hallway, and the other led to the county jail, where only the hardened expressions of those familiar with its routines betrayed any sign of life.

Stories of hauntings had circulated in the small town for years, but now the old abandoned prison was open to the public. A neon green sign out front advertised a "haunted history" tour that ran every Friday night for $29 per person. Inside, the dark walls were damp with age and the air filled with a feeling of dread. The tours could only run if no one was incarcerated in one of the jail cells, but of course, no one ever was.

The old jail was eerily quiet on Fridays. If there was someone in the old jail and no chance of them being released before the tour started, they'd be shuffled over to the sheriff's station for the weekend.

Blue turned away from the square, clicked the lock button on her key fob, and headed into Sucre Bleu. On her way in, she had to pass Lunatic Fringe, the best salon in town, and an empty space for rent. The building next to Blue's shop, the empty one for rent, was super-duper haunted, and no one local would rent it. Especially not after the infamous Hemlock Hollow Ice Cream Social incident two years before.

Blue quickly glanced up and down the street as she passed, refusing to look directly into the windows. No matter how hard she tried, she couldn't shake her superstitions;

witches were famously superstitious for a reason. As a chill ran down her spine, she hurried along, wishing she could have avoided the building altogether.

The silver doorbell tinkled as the doors opened, instantly lifting the heavy weight of the spooky atmosphere outside. The sweet smell of sugar and soft lights welcomed everyone who entered Sucre Blue like a warm hug. Blue had worked hard to create a calming atmosphere; every corner was filled with soft music and inviting décor. Customers were drawn in by the combination of bright colors, playful décor and warm smiles, and left feeling like they'd just spent time with family. Sales of candy and other treats soared, but Blue knew it was more than just a business, it was the perfect place for customers to feel like they belonged.

Blue stepped inside and flipped on the lights, illuminating pink and white checkered floors that still gleamed from their mopping the night before. Her eyes swept the room, taking in the striped designs of the walls and ceiling. A pink and white floral centerpiece sat on the showcase countertop in front of her, its colors complementing the room's decorations perfectly. The glass cases in front of her shone in the morning light streaming through the huge plate glass windows, which surrounded her cozy corner shop.

All she had to do was pull the day's stock from the walk-in cooler in the back and turn on the coffee pot. Once that was done, she leaned on the counter and watched the coffee percolate into the pot. Her mouth watered from the prospect of a piping hot cup of joe. Blue looked over at the spot where the cream and sugar normally sat and realized she hadn't put them out yet.

She pulled the door of the walk-in cooler open, and a rush of cold air filled her nostrils as she scanned the shelves for the containers of cream and sugar. After restocking the condiments to their proper places, she grabbed a box of filter paper and spooned coffee into the filter basket. As she watched the dark beans slowly percolate into the pot, she could almost taste the aroma of the freshly brewed coffee in her mouth.

Blue quickly checked to make sure her preparations were complete, ready for her customers. As she was setting up the ones on the customer side, she heard a deep rumbling noise.

She recognized the sound of a motorcycle, a rarity in the sleepy village, and spun around to look out the window. A sleek black bike glided into the empty spot in front of the abandoned building next door. The man atop it wore a shiny chrome half-helmet and, once parked, unstrapped it from beneath his chin and tucked it gently into a gleaming leather saddlebag.

Blue's eyes were wide with awe as the man before her shook his thick, auburn mane. His hair was slightly tousled, a carefully cultivated bedhead look that gave him a slightly rockstar-esque vibe. If Bon Jovi had been half as striking, she thought to herself. Suddenly, Blue felt the heat of embarrassment rise in her cheeks as she realized she'd been openly staring at him.

He slowly ran his fingers through his auburn hair, and Blue caught her breath as she watched the muscles of his arm flex. When his gaze met hers, a jolt of recognition passed through her.

She yelped and threw herself to the side, desperately searching for a hiding spot. Unfortunately, the giant plate glass window ensured she was completely on display and her reflexive motion only caused her to crash onto the floor with a thud. Her face flushed red with embarrassment as she realized it was the second time that day she'd ended up in that exact position…

At the risk of total and devastating humiliation, she glanced back out the window. The man rocked back and forth on the balls of his feet, shifting from one foot to the other, looking at her as if silently asking himself whether he should come to her aid.

She hesitated for a moment and then, feeling a strange bit of courage, threw her thumb up in the air and smiled. The man's face broke out into a wide smile and he nodded in her direction. Blue turned herself over on all fours and crawled off to die of embarrassment.

Chapter Two

Blue stared at her phone, groaning as she read the email from one of her suppliers. She had forgotten her laptop in the car, and now she would have to go retrieve it if she wanted to answer the email with any kind of efficiency. With a sigh, she grabbed her keys and got ready to go.

She had to walk past the empty storefront. She peered nervously out the window and saw the large motorcycle parked out front. As she walked by, Blue could make out a figure through the dusty window, but she couldn't tell if it was the same person she had seen in there before. The doors to the beauty salon next door were open, and music from within spilled onto the street. Maybe he was in there.

His hair was fabulous…

But, unless he'd been there for a serious overhaul, there's no way his appointment at Lunatic Fringe would have lasted so long. Blue realized that standing at the window speculating wasn't going to get her computer in her hands. She needed to hurry while there weren't any customers, so Blue headed out the door. Seconds later, she had her answer.

The man had taped a sheet of crinkled white printer paper to the door, the words "Moore Investigations" typed in a bold font. For a moment, she considered entering the building and introducing herself to the man, but quickly remembered their first meeting… where she had stumbled and landed on her butt in front of him. Embarrassed and feeling slightly defeated, she grabbed her laptop from the backseat of her car and made her way back towards her shop.

Just as Blue was about to pass Moore Investigations, a tall figure stepped out onto the sidewalk. His eyes lit up with recognition, his lips pulled back in a wide grin, and Blue felt her insides do a backflip.

She took a few seconds to look him up and down, her gaze resting on his strong jawline and eyes that seemed to sparkle like sapphires. His face had a familiar, almost unreal quality to it, as if he'd slipped through the pages of a glossy magazine and into the quaint streets of Hemlock Hollow. She nearly rolled her eyes.

But there he was. His lips quivered as his beaming smile morphed into a nervous grin and he ran his fingers over the patch of scruff on his chin. He cocked his head and asked, "Did I miss something? Is there something on my face?"

Blue was staring at him again. She was being such a complete weirdo that she'd made the poor man think there was something wrong with his perfect face.

"No, sorry. Sorry. I was just lost in thought."

He let out a deep, throaty chuckle, and Blue felt a wave of butterflies in her stomach. She stepped back, her cheeks burning, and looked away. She had to get out of there before she made an even bigger fool of herself.

"I'm Ethan Moore." He extended his hand to her. "I've just moved in next door. Well, my business anyway. I am new in town too, I guess."

Blue and Ethan locked eyes, and Blue could for sure tell he was nervous. His face had a hint of flush, and he stumbled over his words, like a schoolboy trying to talk to his first crush. He fiddled with his shirt collar, looked away, and then back at her again.

Blue kept her gaze straight ahead, though she felt Ethan's eyes linger on her face every few moments. She could feel the faintest of blushes creep onto her cheeks too and hoped he didn't notice. She refused to acknowledge that her heart seemed to skip a beat whenever she flicked her eyes up to find him still watching her. No, certainly not. A meet cute like this only happened in the movies.

A thought started to niggle at the back of Blue's mind. Was she still at the bottom of her basement stairs? Was the entire day some sort of hallucination brought on by a concussion? That would certainly explain things.

Time seemed to stand still as she placed her hand in Ethan's. His grip was strong and secure, but his palm was warm and gentle. As their fingers brushed together, a jolt of electricity ran through her and she felt her insides flutter with anticipation.

Blue pulled her hand away afraid that Ethan would feel the increase in her pulse. "I'm Blue," she managed before…

The sound of a man's voice shouting, "Blue! Blue Bell!" jerked her out of the trance she had been in daydreaming about Ethan Moore and his motorcycle. She looked up to see a gruff-looking man with graying hair waiting impatiently. He barked at her, "Are you going to stand there all day? You are supposed to have my order ready!"

"I'm sorry, I have to go," Blue apologized.

"Who is that guy?" Ethan asked with a grunt.

"Tom Wiseman. Jellybean order," she said and then rushed off. "Nice to meet you, Ethan," Blue said it over her shoulder just before disappearing into Sucre Bleu.

Tom Wiseman paced back and forth in front of the shop counter, his face flushed and anger radiating from him. He let out an exasperated sigh and slammed his fist down on the counter. "I can't believe I've had to wait this long," he grumbled.

Blue was used to Tom being unpleasant. Everyone was used to Tom being unpleasant. She wasn't even sure why he kept coming to Sucre Bleu, because he was always unhappy with either her candy or her service. She supposed it was because she was the only candy maker in the area. They were forced into an unhappy and uncomfortable business arrangement.

"I'm sorry, I just stepped out for a moment," Blue said apologetically, turning towards the back of the shop. "Let me just go grab it from the back."

Tom's face reddened further and his fists clenched tight as he bellowed, "Now wait just one second!" The force of his voice was much louder than his usual belligerence level.

Blue wondered if he was drunk or something. She turned around to face him and tried not to sigh or roll her eyes. Deep down, she knew that would only set him off further.

Fail on both accounts.

"You know what, I don't think I want that order. I can just get some candy off Amazon or something. I want a refund."

Blue swallowed hard and fixed a smile on her face. "I'm sorry, but I can't refund any custom orders." She felt her temples begin to throb as her knuckles turned white from gripping the counter.

Tom's face hardened and he stepped closer, his words becoming more pointed and inappropriate with each passing statement. Blue's jaw tightened and her eyes narrowed. She kept her fists balled at her sides, willing herself to remain composed as the barrage of insults continued.

But then he said something about her and her high-school-aged sister... a backhanded jab about them strutting around town like common sluts, exploiting their looks and barely staying in business. Shock and rage washed over her in an icy wave.

Her nails dug into her palms, and the words flew out of her mouth like venom from a cobra. "I'd come across this counter and wring your neck myself if I wasn't wearing heels!" At that very moment, the old-fashioned bells over the doors tinkled cheerfully, as if mocking her outburst.

Ethan Moore was at the head of the small line of customers filing into the store, and he visibly cringed when he heard what she said. The two women who walked in behind him looked equally horrified, but their shock was soon forgotten as the specials board caught their eye.

Ethan's long legs quickly carried him across the store, and he put himself between Tom and Blue. "Leave now."

"This is none of your business, young man. This… woman, if you can really call her that, owes me a refund, and I will not budge until I get it."

Ethan stepped closer and towered over Tom, his eyes blazing with anger. "I said leave. Now." His voice was a low rumble.

"What? Who do you think you are?" Tom spluttered. He dug his hand into his pocket and pulled out his phone, waving it in Ethan's face. "I'm calling the cops! She just threatened to kill me! You heard her, you're my witness!"

"Sir, you really need to leave." Ethan repeated it without so much as flinch of reaction, but Blue could hear the undercurrent of menace in his voice. There was a warning there, and Tom picked up on it too.

He weighed the two options silently, his eyes darting between Blue and Ethan. Finally, he bowed his head in defeat and mumbled, "Fine. Can I have my jellybean order?" His voice was small, as if he expected to be scolded for even daring to ask. His shoulders were slumped, and his face had taken on a lost, dejected expression.

Blue dashed to the back of the store, snatched up two boxes of grape jellybeans, and rushed back to the front. Tom's face sagged, his eyes wide and lips quivering, while Ethan towered over him with his arms folded tightly across his chest.

She placed the boxes on the smooth glass countertop, her fingers running over the gold foil wrapping. Out of the corner of her eye, she saw that Ethan's gaze was firmly fixed on Tom, who seemed to be frozen in place. After a few moments of silence, Tom finally reached out and took the jellybeans, his knuckles white against the brightly colored packaging, and quickly made his way out of the store.

Ethan silently trailed Tom out of the store, his eyes glued to the back of his head. Blue watched them with a breath stuck in her chest, hoping Ethan was just ensuring Tom left for good and wasn't going to beat him up once they were outside. Not that Tom didn't deserve some lumps, but Blue shook her head... Ethan just didn't put out a violent vibe.

Ethan paused with his hand on the door handle as he looked at her. "Well, if you need anything," he said, flashing a gentle smile, "you know where to find me." He slowly closed the door behind himself, leaving her alone with the two ladies who'd followed him in.

The women held their breath as they watched the men leave the shop. When they were finally gone, one of them let out a sigh of relief and exclaimed, "Oh my goodness!"

With the excitement over, Blue realized who the ladies were. It was Mel and Tonya Carson, who were famous around town for their emotional roller coaster of overeating and unhealthy habits followed by strict diet and exercise regimens. Both had round faces, bright eyes, and charismatic smiles, each topped off with a different color of lipstick, but only when it wasn't being smudged off with a quick lick of their fingers after another indulgent bite.

Blue was out for a walk one day when, to her surprise, she spotted two people jogging side by side, each wearing athletic shorts and a tank top. Those two people were the Carson sisters. They were snacking on chocolate-covered strawberries, held in a clear plastic container which they passed back and forth. It was a strange sight, yet it paid off. Within two weeks of seeing them, Blue had sold out of strawberries every single day.

Mel and Tonya must have been in the indulgent phase of their cycle. They both positively buzzed with excitement, and Blue couldn't help but be a little jazzed about the impending huge sale.

Blue gave them a strained smile as she approached and asked, "What can I get you ladies today?" She could feel the awkwardness of the previous incident with Tom hanging in the air and hoped they would just forget about it.

"Who was that hunk of beefcake that led Tom out of here like a dog?" Mel asked, because of course she wasn't going to just let it go.

But Blue had misread their shock after the incident. They weren't focused on Tom. Oh, no, they only had eyes for Ethan. Which Blue could more than understand but didn't want to dwell on any longer.

"He's moved into the building next door," was Blue's reply. "There's a sign on the door that says 'Moore Investigations'. I think he's a private investigator. He seemed nice, though I only met him briefly."

Tonya's eyebrows shot up and a sly smile crept across her lips. "Oh, only met him briefly, huh?" She paused, enjoying the moment of suspense before continuing breathlessly, "Well, you must have made quite the impression on him if he was over here ready to defend your honor."

Blue bit her lip and stared down at the floor, choosing her words carefully. "That's not exactly what happened," she said slowly. "He must have just stopped in for some candy and happened to see Tom acting like a total jerk. That's all." She could feel the weight of her own words as she said them, knowing that she was only half-telling the truth.

"Right," Mel said.

"He's definitely some sort of law enforcement." Tonya had turned to her sister at that point.

The sisters nattered and giggled as they examined the selection of lollipops, caramels and gumdrops behind the glass counter, their comments about Ethan and his toned arms filling the air. Blue shifted from one foot to the other, trying not to eavesdrop. What she really wanted was to stop thinking about Ethan, and the Carson sisters were not making that easy.

"I think we're ready," Mel said after a couple of minutes.

Blue quickly and efficiently boxed up their order and handed it over the counter. The sisters handed Blue the exact change and thanked her for her help. But as she prepared to turn away and head into the back the sisters made it clear they weren't ready to move on just yet.

Chapter Three

After ten minutes of Mel and Tonya pressing Blue about Ethan Moore, they finally left the candy store. Blue struggled to stay cheerful during the interrogation, but the Carson sisters were some of her best customers, so she kept her happy, smiling, customer service face on throughout their questions.

The rest of the morning passed mostly uneventfully. A while after the Carson sisters left, Pepper came bouncing into the shop.

Blue's eyes narrowed as she glanced at her wristwatch and gestured to the street. "Aren't you supposed to be in class right now?" Her words were an accusation, and there was a look of disappointment in her eyes.

"It's early day." Pepper didn't miss a beat, and it got Blue hot under the collar.

"No, it isn't. That's tomorrow. You're skipping school."

"So, it's just social studies. I'm a senior now. It's practically an obligation for me to skip."

Blue opened her mouth to speak, but her stomach suddenly growled loudly, echoing in the room like a roaring lion. A pang of hunger shot through her, reminding her that she'd hardly eaten anything all day; she'd had only a few bites of a waffle for breakfast and numerous cups of coffee since then.

"Me too." Pepper answered Blue's stomach. "What's for dinner tonight, sis?"

Blue surveyed the shop. There wasn't much there that would masquerade as a real meal, but the cupboards were bare at home. There might have been a few scrapes of peanut butter left in the jar and a slice or two of not-too-stale bread. Blue didn't like to admit that the waffles she'd given Pepper for breakfast had been the last of their real food.

"Peanut butter sandwiches?" Blue asked hopefully.

Pepper heaved an exaggerated sigh and slumped her shoulders, holding the pose with a dramatic flair. Her eyes were wide, and her lower lip was sticking out, the signature expression of teenage exasperation. Blue took notice and couldn't help but feel a trace of annoyance, but she couldn't get too angry Pepper had learned it from her older sister...

"I'll run over to the general store and get some groceries." Pepper nodded out the window toward the store across the square.

"About that..." Blue tried to figure out how to tell her sister that they didn't exactly have a lot of money for groceries... or any at all.

"How are we still broke?" Pepper asked. "This is one of the most popular stores in town. How are we not rich? We should be rolling in dough."

"Candy doesn't have a huge margin," Blue said, but she hated discussing money with Pepper. Kids shouldn't have to worry about such things, but Pepper was nearly an adult. Plus, their precarious financial situation directly affected her too. When they only had enough money for stale peanut butter sandwiches or candy for dinner, Pepper had to deal with it too.

"I'll just play the Quick Pick," Pepper said. "All I need is a couple of bucks, and we'll be set for groceries."

"You can't," Blue said.

"What choice do we have, Blue? There's no food in the house, and my meal card ran out at school today. You can't starve a growing teenager."

"But…" But Blue cut herself off. Pepper was right. "Fine. Play the Quick Pick, but don't win too big."

"Why not? Why can't we live a little?" Pepper complained. "We're witches after all…"

"Because using magic for personal gain is wrong, and there will be consequences. You know this. Just enough to get by, and we'll probably be fine. But you have to keep your winning on the down low. And for the same reason we're broke. You know this stuff. Even though I wish you didn't."

"Dad's debts," Pepper said. "I know. I'm sorry."

"It's not like he owed a credit card company or a doctor's office. The men he owes money to are bad. We have to stay under the radar."

"Just a little win. Enough to get some food and some money for my meal card," Pepper said.

"Yes, thank you, sis."

"And maybe a lipstick? Just one?"

Blue was about to tell her no, but she couldn't bring herself to do it. She couldn't imagine being a teenage girl and not being able to buy the occasional lipstick or other small luxury. Especially since when she was a teenager, they still had all of her father's dirty money. Her teenage years had been a lot more extravagant that Pepper's would ever be, and for some reason, that made Blue feel incredibly guilty.

"One lipstick. And make sure you get some vegetables. A little broccoli wouldn't hurt us every now and again."

"Ew."

"Pepper."

"Fine. I'm getting the kind with cheese sauce, though."

"Sounds good to me," Blue replied. Cheese sauce literally made everything better.

Pepper grabbed her purse and reusable shopping bags, and with a wave, she exited out the front door. Blue watched her go, then turned and headed to the back of the store. She slipped into a clean white apron and flipped on the light switch to reveal a counter full of tools and ingredients for the custom chocolate order she was about to start.

An hour later, Blue emerged for a last cup of coffee. Out the window, she could see Pepper coming across the street weighed down with grocery bags. Blue grabbed her key fob and unlocked the door so Pepper could load the groceries into the car.

She watched Pepper drop everything into the back seat and head back towards the shop. The sisters quickly cleaned up for the evening and closed the store.

"Can I drive home?" Pepper asked as Blue locked up.

"You don't have a license. Remember when you failed driver's ed?"

"I had the flu. Puking on the instructor shouldn't be a reason to fail. I was robbed."

"And when you failed again junior year?"

"My guidance counselor said they can squeeze me in next semester. I should be able to get my license before I graduate," Pepper replied.

"Well, when you do, we'll talk about you driving my car."

"You're no fun."

"You're really not going to think I'm fun when we talk about how you have to get a part-time job because I cannot afford to add a teenager to my insurance."

"I don't see why we need insurance anyway." Pepper slumped into the passenger seat and rolled her eyes. "Even if we get in an accident, we can just fix it with magic."

"It's not that easy, Pep. You know that. We're limited with what we can do."

"I think we could be far more powerful if we spent actual time practicing."

"Even if we were, we couldn't use it." Blue started the car and backed out of her space. "We're limited by our circumstances, so we might as well focus on real life. We've got bigger problems."

"That being all powerful witches could fix," Pepper protested.

"That kind of power just brings more problems."

"Blue, I just don't believe you."

"Ouch."

"I'm sorry," Pepper said. "I know you're just trying to do what's best for me, but I think you're selling us short. How many people would give a kidney to be witches, and we just ignore it in favor of paying bills and... I don't know... yard work."

Blue looked down at the steering wheel and tried to ignore the lump in her throat. She felt like a jailer as she tried to explain why her sister was not allowed to do things that other witches did without a second thought. Blue hated herself for having imposed the restrictions, but she knew it was for the best.

They arrived home a couple of minutes later after a short drive full of stony quiet, and Blue helped Pepper carry the groceries in. The two of them put the food away in silence. Blue left the comments about their avoidance of magic hanging in the air.

"We've got several options here," Blue said once everything was put away. "What should we make?"

"I've got a science test tomorrow. I need to study." Pepper sulked. She'd obviously been hoping that her comments about magic would prod Blue into a little spell-casting practice.

"Okay. Well, I'll make burgers, and I'll let you know when they're ready."

"Fiiiiine."

As Blue put the patties on the griddle, Tiffany sauntered into the kitchen. "Ugh. Burgers again? Gag me with a spoon!"

"You could always just have cat food." Blue was in no mood for the familiar's complaining.

"Ew. As if!"

Blue shot Tiffany a look.

"As long as there's no pickles on mine. Pickles are so gross."

"I was just going to cut up your hamburger patty and put it in your bowl. Just like I always do. Pickles were never going to be an issue."

"Pickles are always an issue." Tiffany sat down across the kitchen from Blue and started cleaning her paw.

Blue took a deep breath and exhaled slowly, trying to push all of her worries aside for the moment. All she wanted was to make it through dinner and then indulge in a mindless movie. She had watched her favorite one so many times that she could practically quote it, but it was comforting and the perfect way to wind down from the day.

The dinner table was empty and quiet, save for the clinking of Blue's silverware on her plate as she ate her broccoli in cheddar sauce. Pepper had taken her meal and retreated to her room, her shoulders slumped in angst. Blue remembered she'd left her laptop at the shop. And their home PC was fried.

For a brief moment, she contemplated asking Pepper if she could borrow her laptop. All she needed to do was check the message from the supplier and digitally sign off. But Pepper was allegedly studying for a science exam. In case that was true, Blue decided it was best to leave her alone.

She tied her shoes with a double knot, grabbed her keys and wallet, and trudged out the door. She had planned to spend the evening sprawled out on the couch, but instead here she was, heading back into work.

Chapter Four

Blue wondered why Ethan would leave trash outside of his office like that? Surely the landlord told him what day garbage day was, and where had he gotten two large bags of trash in the few hours since she'd left work? Surely private investigation didn't produce much refuse. The building had been empty, if not dusty, as far as Blue knew, so it's not like he had to clean the office out when he moved in.

As she stepped closer to the garbage bags, Blue realized they weren't garbage bags at all. She stood there on the sidewalk frozen because what she looked at was impossible…

Right?

Once it registered that her eyes were telling her the truth, she pulled her phone out of her purse. Her hands shook as she dialed.

Blue's heart raced as the dispatcher told her to stay put, lock the doors and not to leave. She quickly scrambled back into her car and locked the door, her hands trembling as she fumbled with the keys.

While she spoke with dispatch and waited for the sheriff's department, she did something she hadn't done in a long time. Blue drew a small protection sigil in the dust on her car door just under the window. A thin layer of dust had built up on the dashboard and windows of the car. Blue picked up an old pen, left the cap on, and carefully wrote a small charm in the dust on the driver's side window. She blew away the excess dust, watching as the carved letters sparkled in the streetlight.

Her other hand gripped the phone as she stared out the front windshield. In the moment, she was glad Pepper was mad at her and hadn't begged to come along. She couldn't imagine stumbling over a dead body with her sister in tow.

"What's that?" the dispatcher asked. "Ma'am, are you okay?"

It was then Blue realized she was chanting a spell to go along with the sigil. She was casting without even thinking about it.

"Oh, yes. Just a little mantra to calm my anxiety."

The dispatcher chuckled. "I do that, too. Works like a charm. Hey, do you see the sheriff's deputies? I have their location, and you should see the lights."

Blue looked on out the windshield again, and she did see the lights. "Yes, I see them. They don't have their sirens on."

"In case the killer is still around, dear. That's why you're locked in your car. You're still locked in your car, right?"

"Yes."

"Good, don't get out until I confirmed with the deputy that arrives first."

Once that was done, Blue hung up with the dispatcher and stumbled out of the car, her jaw dropping as she took in the unfolding scene. Police officers descended upon a body, barricades blocking off the entrance to Moore Investigations. She refused to look towards it, instead collapsing onto the curb in front of her shop.

She kept waiting for someone to come over and tell her what was going on or at least ask her questions. But everyone was too busy. They were all wrapped up in their work, and she'd just have to wait until someone was ready for her.

Undersheriff McKinley had looked over at her a few times and offered a reassuring nod. They'd been friends for a long time, but even he was in no hurry to get to her.

Blue had sent Pepper a text message telling her that she'd be out for a while. Pepper's response had been, 'Have fun and be safe.'

Blue didn't have the heart to tell her what was really going on, but Pepper's lack of questions worried her too. If Pepper wasn't curious about what Blue was up to, then that meant the teenager was up to something. As long as Tiffany was there, Blue's familiar would keep the girl somewhat in line.

Maybe…

Blue felt like she was operating in a dream state. Her thoughts floated by her like wisps of smoke, too insubstantial to be grasped. Her head throbbed with a dull pain, and an ache seemed to settle in her chest. Nothing that happened around her could penetrate the thick fog of her traumatized mind.

Had she ever even seen a dead body before? A few times, but at funerals in the quiet darkness of the funeral home. But this was different. It was Tom, lying on the cold ground with nothing behind his eyes. His expressionless face haunted her, still carrying the same determined look from when she'd seen him alive hours before.

The telltale rumble of a motorcycle engine pierced the air, and she glanced up to see Ethan skidding to a stop on the other side of the shop. The street was clogged with law enforcement cruisers and crime scene vehicles, but he managed to find a small opening and squeezed his bike into it. He wore a black leather jacket, giving off an air of nonchalance, but beneath the façade, she could sense his worry.

There was a concerned look etched on his face. He crossed the street with smooth movements, like a panther stalking its prey, and unexpectedly, he sunk down on the curb next to her. "You okay?"

Blue shifted uncomfortably, hesitated for a long moment, and finally said, "Not really," with a barely concealed edge in her voice. She let out a short huff and crossed her arms to fight off a chill that wasn't coming from the air around them.

"What's going on?"

"There's a body outside of your office. I found it when I came back to get my laptop."

Ethan turned his head and surveyed the commotion going on around them. "Yep, that appears to be what's going on."

"What are you doing here? Your arrival is auspicious."

"Don't you mean suspicious?" Ethan cocked a curious eyebrow.

"No, I mean auspicious. I was going out of my mind just sitting here waiting for something to happen. Anyway, what are you doing here?"

"I had a security notification on my phone."

"A security notification?"

"Yeah, that's what I was doing here all day," Ethan said and scooted a fraction of an inch closer to Blue. Protective instincts he hadn't felt for a long time blossomed in his chest and in his gut when he was close to her.

"You were installing a security system?" Blue asked, and she wondered if Ethan had just scooted closer to her.

"Yep. The landlord said it was fine as long as it didn't cost him anything."

"That sounds like him." Blue nodded but stared at the ground.

"So, I spent the day getting that all squared away. It's kind of a necessity in my line of work."

"I can see that."

"But, I was out in my garage working when the alert came in, and of course, my phone was in the house. I hate that thing, so I leave it behind sometimes. Especially when I'm at home."

"That doesn't sound like a good habit for a private investigator."

"Should I get one of those belt holsters like people used to wear back in the '90s?"

A full-body laugh ripped through Blue, so loud that the deputies and crime scene techs turned to look. Blue covered her mouth with one hand and wiped the tears from her eyes with the other. "Sorry," she said when she'd successfully stifled the laugh. "I just… wow. I didn't realize how tense I was."

"Glad I could help." Ethan's smile was genuine and affectionate. Being a witch, Blue could read people well, and Ethan was good. He tried to hide it behind a gruff exterior and a biker aesthetic, but he was a decent human being.

Blue straightened up. "You said there was a security alert. What was it? Do you have cameras or something that caught who did this?"

"My cameras caught a person, but you can't see their face."

He pulled out his phone, swiped his finger across the screen, and held it out for Blue to see. She watched as a compact sedan pulled up to the curb outside Moore Investigations and a figure emerged from the backseat, dragging a limp body behind them. The car doors slammed shut, and the tires screeched as it sped away into the night.

"We have to show this to them." Blue nodded toward the deputies milling around. "Let me make the introductions."

Blue slowly stood up and brushed the dirt off her pants. She glanced warily at Brock as she nervously shuffled her way over to him. Ethan followed discreetly, his hands shoved deep in his pockets.

"Brock… Undersheriff McKinley, this is Ethan Moore. He has some footage from his security camera to show you."

Ethan pulled up the footage on the phone and showed it to Brock. "Do you have this available on a bigger screen?"

"I do. I've got everything recorded in my office."

"Can I take a look?" Brock asked.

Blue watched as Ethan pursed his lips. "I can email it to you to watch at the station."

"I'd like to take a look right now. Time is important."

"I understand that, Undersheriff McKinley, but there's sensitive information in my office. I'm afraid I cannot let you in. Unless you have a warrant."

Brock huffed a breath out through his nose. "Fine, send it to me."

"Right away, sir."

Brock and Ethan exchanged information while Blue stood back. She understood why Ethan wouldn't let the deputies into his office, but she also understood why Brock was annoyed. Her only hope was to stay out of it.

Yeah, right…

Brock and a couple of his deputies headed over to one of the cruisers to watch the footage on one of their laptops. Ethan walked back over to where Blue stood waiting for someone to take her statement so she could go home.

"He's not going to like that," Blue said as soon as Ethan joined her.

"I know." Ethan was a little sheepish, and he rubbed the back of his neck. "I get it too. I would be annoyed with me, but I have a fiduciary duty to my clients. I cannot let law enforcement into my offices without a warrant. Once you let them in, they can poke around in anything, and my clients pay good money for me to make sure that doesn't happen."

"You just moved to town. Like today. You already have an office full of super-secret files?" Blue was mostly joking, but she was also kind of curious too. She figured he wouldn't have any clients yet or cases.

In fact, what was he doing in Hemlock Hollow? Was there really that great of a need for a private detective in their sleepy little town?

"A lot of my business can be done online, Blue. Plus, I'm a plane ride away from anywhere I need to go. I mostly work with clients who can afford that kind of thing."

"So, why did…"

35

"Why did I move to Hemlock Hollow?" he cut her off.

Blue studied his face, searching for any indication as to why he was here. His eyes were set in a neutral expression, but the curve of his mouth seemed to suggest mild amusement. She couldn't tell if he was annoyed or simply trying to calm her fears. Could this be more than her usual paranoia, and he was here for something far more sinister?

She studied his face to see if her gut was wrong. His brow was furrowed, and his lips were pursed. But she got the feeling that his gruff exterior was just a mask, hiding something softer underneath. She trusted her intuition and wanted to know what he was really like when you peeled back his many layers.

"Did you recognize the car?" Ethan answered her question with a question, and she realized she'd been prying.

When you were constantly surrounded by small-town gossip, it was easy to forget that most people didn't want to spill their private business to strangers.

Blue's face flushed and she shuffled her feet, avoiding eye contact. "I'm sorry," she mumbled, her voice barely audible. "I should have known better than to ask so many questions. I didn't mean to be nosy." She studied the cracks in the sidewalk, afraid to look up.

"It's okay, Blue. I would love to tell you all about my life, but not here and not like this. If we're going to get to know each other, and I think we should since we're neighbors… business neighbors anyway, I'd like to do it somewhere other than a crime scene."

"I did not recognize the car." Blue's response was all she could muster. The way he'd talked about them getting to know each other had made her stomach do another stupid flip-flop. And she hated it because she did not have the time or space in her life to go all gooey over a man like Ethan.

No matter how tempting any man, especially one with the blue eyes and chiseled jaw of Ethan Moore, might be, she knew to stay away. He had a way about him, a twinkle in his eye and a knowing smirk on his lips that made her heart race, but she was wise enough to see that look was trouble in the making.

"Blue?"

Blue felt heat rising in her cheeks again as she realized she had been daydreaming again. She knew she blushed way too much around Ethan.

Her eyes darted back and forth as she tried to retrieve her thoughts on the topic before her, her attempts at concentration were no match for the towering image of Ethan in her mind. "Sorry, I was just trying to recall the details of the car," she said, trying to recover from her trance.

"Anything?"

"No. Sorry. What was it? Like a Nissan Accord?"

"You mean a Honda Accord?"

"Yeah, that." Blue didn't really know cars.

"Toyota Corolla."

37

"Oh. Those are super common, right?" Blue may not know much about cars, but she knew that Corollas were one of the most common cars out there.

"Indeed, and there were no plates." Ethan rubbed his chin. "If only the killer had been a classic car enthusiast."

"Maybe they are, and they knew better than to drive one to a body dump."

"That's a pretty good observation," Ethan admitted. "Have you ever worked in law enforcement?"

"No. I make candy. And sell the candy."

A deep, hearty laugh rolled out of Ethan's chest and into Blue's ears, sending a pleasant shiver down her spine. His eyes sparkled and his mouth quirked up at the corners. She found herself wishing he'd laugh like this more often. "Well, you're observant and a natural problem solver."

"Essential skills for candy making and selling."

His shoulders shook with laughter, and she felt a smile tugging at her lips. Was this banter? She glanced around the crime scene; officers were still darting between the yellow tape and gathering evidence. Tom Wiseman's body was still lying on the ground, and the reality of their situation swept away her good humor.

Chapter Five

A tired-looking officer took down her statement, and Blue was finally free to go home. As she stepped through the threshold, she found Pepper draped on the couch, laughter spilling from her lips as she watched some cheesy reality show with Tiffany. She paused for a moment, surveying the scene with a heavy sigh.

"Hey, guys." Blue plopped down next to them.

"I want to go to the mall." Tiffany stood up and stretched.

"It's closed," Pepper said so Blue didn't have to.

"You two are the worst," Tiffany groused, "to say the least."

The familiar jumped off the sofa and darted down the hall toward the kitchen. "I'll feed her," Pepper said and pushed off the couch too. "When she finds out her food bowl is half empty, she'll be back in here complaining again."

"I'll come too. I think I'm going to make myself an old-fashioned."

"Can I have one?" Pepper asked hopefully.

"Absolutely not. But you can have a maraschino cherry for your soda."

"You're the worst." Pepper sulked down the hall.

"I'm just trying to be responsible," Blue said. "And by the way, you sound like Tiffany."

"You're my sister, not my mom." Pepper shook some food into Tiffany's bowl, ignoring Blue's comment.

The cat, sensing the tension between the sisters and fur standing on end, meowed in alarm and darted out of the room. Blue watched her go with a pang of envy. Why couldn't she just dive into her bed, too?

Pepper watched as Blue reached for a crystal highball glass, the light from the kitchen window glinting off its facets. Her sister's deft hands expertly mixed crushed ice and a splash of bitters with her favorite whiskey. After that, Blue added some sugar and a bit of water. Without turning around, Pepper leaned back against the cool robin's egg blue laminate counter and met Blue's gaze with a steady glare.

Blue surveyed the kitchen. The outdated laminate counters were stamped with a small paisley pattern, and the cabinets had recently been refinished but still seemed to belong to a different time. The appliances were clean but, despite their care, were as outdated as the rest of the room. Blue sighed, knowing that she would have to wait to turn her visions of a modern updated kitchen into reality. Updating the kitchen was on the top of Blue's list of things to do once she had enough money to do anything.

Who knew when that would be, though… Or perhaps someday their parents would resurface, and she'd have to buy herself a new house. That was doubtful, though, so for the foreseeable future, the house she'd grown up in was her permanent abode. At least it was paid for. As long as she could keep up on the taxes, she and Pepper never had to worry about being homeless.

Blue finally spoke after she'd finished adding a few more drops of whiskey to her glass and stirring it with a delicate clink of ice cubes. She dropped two shiny maraschino cherries into Pepper's glass of Coke and grabbed both beverages, walking over to the kitchen table. She sat down and met Pepper's eyes. "I know I'm not Mom," she said softly.

Pepper eventually joined her. "So, how was your date?"

"Oh, I wasn't on a date." Blue barked out an uncomfortable laugh. "I went back to the shop to grab my laptop, and I practically tripped over Tom Wiseman."

"What? What was Tom doing at the shop?"

"He wasn't. He was dead in front of Moore Investigations." Blue took another pull of her drink.

"Oh, my gawd. Did that hot biker guy kill him?"

Blue narrowed her eyes at her sister. What did she know about Ethan? "Have you met him?"

"No, I just saw him through the window. He's smokin'. I had hoped for your sake that's where you were."

"I did see him. He came by while I was waiting to give my statement. He got a hit on his security system. Had the killer on video."

"Oh, good. Who was it?"

"Couldn't see their face. They drove up in a Toyota Corolla with no license plate. Do you know anybody who drives a Corolla?"

"What year?" Pepper asked.

"Older. Not sure."

"What color?"

"Couldn't tell because it was dark, but probably beige or gray."

"Blue, half of my school drives older Corollas that are gray or beige. That's like the most common car ever."

"I know," Blue said with a sigh. "So, I guess there's a killer on the loose in Hemlock Hollow."

"It was probably that Ethan guy, Blue. He's hot, but he's new in town."

"I don't think it was him, Pepper."

"Why? Because he's hot? I don't think anybody has ever been murdered in this town, and the day he shows up, someone gets killed? It's too big of a coincidence to overlook."

"I got a pretty good read on him. He's a good man. Ethan Moore is not a killer, Pepper."

"Oh my gosh, did you use magic? On him? Are we finally using magic?"

Blue thought Pepper was way too excited. "It was just my intuition. No big deal." Blue wondered if she should tell Pepper about the sigil or her unconscious spell chanting. "I did do a little magic, though. When I was in the car waiting for the sheriff's department to arrive, I drew a protection sigil on the car door, and I did a little protection spell chant without even really thinking about it." Blue thought it felt good to admit it.

But Pepper's face softened, as if she had just found something she had been searching for. Her voice was full of wonder as she said, "I knew it! Of all the witches in the world, I had to get stuck with a sister who denied her abilities. But look at you, Blue! You can't fight it any longer - that power inside of you is too strong. You're practically glowing with it."

Blue's voice was resigned, and her eyes clouded over with sadness as she mumbled, "All it took was for a guy to die."

"That sucks, but it's good for you. It's good for us. Can you imagine what we could do if we stopped denying who we really are?"

"You need to calm down, Pepper. Maybe I shouldn't have told you. We cannot go off halfcocked doing magic all the time. You know the stakes."

"I don't think it would have mattered if you told me or not. The magic wants to flow through you. I don't think you can hold it back anymore."

Blue felt a chill go down her spine as she processed the implications of what Pepper was saying. If she was right, then this could turn into a complete catastrophe. If the wrong people found out about their magical abilities, they would be in serious trouble - maybe even risking their lives. They had to remain stealthy and use their powers wisely if they wanted to survive.

Blue's chest tightened and she bit her lip, torn between her moral convictions and the desire to make her sister happy. Pepper's arguments were persuasive, and Blue couldn't help but wonder if her hardline stance against magic was really doing more harm than good. What if, just this once, she let down her guard and allowed Pepper to enjoy the same quality of life that she would without her strict rules?

"A little bit here and there," Blue relented. "But you have to keep it under wraps at school. Promise me."

"You don't need to worry about that, Blue. You remember high school kids, right? If they even get the slightest whiff that I'm different in any way, it would be like piranha feeding time at the zoo."

Blue remembered the torture of trying to fit in at high school and felt a surge of relief when Pepper promised that she would keep their secret in the presence of the "normal" kids. Her face lit up with a mischievous grin. "Maybe this weekend, we'll get Grandma's book out of the attic."

Pepper leapt off the couch, mumbled an excited yelp, and then kissed Blue on top of her head. "You're the absolute best," she said. She glanced over at her school bag in the corner, a poor attempt to remind herself of the science test that was looming in the morning. "Guess I'd better hit the hay. I really do have a test tomorrow."

Blue stood in the hall, watching her little sister Pepper twirl and spin with reckless abandon, smiling and laughing as she danced excitedly down the hall toward her room. Despite Pepper's occasional surly and demanding behavior, Blue couldn't help but feel proud of her. She remembered being full of that same rebellious energy as a teenager towards her beloved Gran.

The memories of Gran's warm embrace and gentle voice seemed to twist in her stomach like a knife. When she thought of Gran, an all-encompassing ache threatened to consume her. Sometimes she missed Gran so much she thought it would eat a hole in her.

At least she knew Gran wasn't gone forever. There was comfort in knowing that they would see her again someday. That was insight that most people didn't have. The comforting knowledge that one day they would see Gran again was something most people would never know… a privilege only witches enjoyed.

So, maybe it was time for Blue to be true herself. What could go wrong?

***

The sun was just beginning to rise when Pepper padded into the kitchen. She switched on the lights and began to prepare breakfast. The percolating coffee soon filled the room with its strong and inviting aroma. Two slices of toast were buttered and ready on a plate, sitting next to an old yellow mug. When Blue emerged from her bedroom, Pepper welcomed her with a warm smile and a cup of steaming coffee.

"Why don't I make eggs to go with the toast?" Blue offered.

"Scrambled with cheese?"

"We'll eat breakfast like kings today."

Pepper rushed through her breakfast, then grabbed her backpack and sprinted outside in time to make the school bus. Blue frantically searched the house for her laptop and muttered under her breath, "If I don't find this stupid thing before I leave, I'm going to have to start stapling it to myself."

While she was retrieving it from the coffee table in the living room, Tiffany wandered in.

"We're not going to the mall." Blue hoped to cut off an argument with her familiar before it even started. "I have to go to work."

"I wasn't going to ask."

"Sure."

"Like fer sure," Tiffany snarked back. "But, like, I totally heard you talking to Pepper about breaking out the family grimoire. And that's like totally fine, like for sure, but are you like for sure?"

"I am like totally for sure," Blue teased Tiffany.

"You don't have to be rude." Tiffany dropped her Valley girl accent and affect. Sometimes she did that. It made Blue wonder if it was even real.

"Sorry, Tiff. Anyway, yes, I'm serious. I'm going to get Gran's spell book. Are you scared?"

"Of magic? No. You doing magic, like totally."

"It will be fine. It's what I was born to do, right?"

"Whatevs."

Tiffany seemed to have said her piece, so Blue grabbed her laptop and headed out.

Chapters Six

Blue had half expected Ethan to be waiting for her when she got to the shop, or maybe she was hoping…

But that made no sense. Why would he be waiting for her, and wouldn't that be kinda creepy?

Ethan actually wasn't around at all. His bike wasn't parked on the street, and his office was dark.

As she unlocked the door to Sucre Bleu, Blue wondered if she'd dreamed him, and if Tom's murder had just been a nightmare. But twenty minutes after she opened, Brock came into the shop, and that idea was out the window.

"I suppose this isn't just a friendly visit," Blue said. "Coffee?"

"Yes, coffee, please. The stuff at the station is dreck."

"And the social call?"

"Afraid not, Blue."

Blue filled two paper cups with the shop's signature blend of dark roast and added liberal amounts of cream and sugar to Brock's. They crossed the happy pink floor to one of the shop's two small tables and chose the one angled just so in front of a large side window, allowing natural light to spill in and warm their faces.

"So, what is it, Brock?"

"I need to know your whereabouts for the three hours before you found the body, Blue."

"What? Like an alibi?" Blue's stomach flipped, but not in the good way like when she saw Ethan. "Why three hours?"

"Something about rigor mortis or something. The coroner can tell he died within three hours prior to you finding him because of stiffness." Brock shivered.

Blue could tell he was uncomfortable talking about such things. She didn't press the issue.

"I was with Pepper."

"Anyone not in your family who can attest to your whereabouts for that three hours?"

"Oh, my gosh, Brock. You cannot be serious. Am I really a suspect?"

"Right now, Blue, you're the only suspect."

Her eyes widened and she blurted out, "What! What about Ethan?" Immediately her heart sank, and a wave of guilt washed over her. She didn't mean it, it just slipped out. She knew Ethan was innocent, but now it was too late. Her shoulders slumped and a lump formed in her throat as she realized what she had potentially done. The last thing she wanted to do was get Ethan in trouble, because she was sure he didn't do it.

"His neighbor completely accounts for his whereabouts during that time. And we have video of him at the shop and leaving. He's cleared."

"Well, that's good at least," Blue said.

"Why?"

She had to think fast of something other than, well, I think he's totally hot. Oh, and I'm a witch and I can read people, so I know he's not guilty.

"He's new in town, so everyone is going to suspect him. If you've cleared him, then he should be fine."

"People are still going to talk given where the body was found, but it is good for him. It's not good for you, Blue."

"It's just… I can't believe you're actually serious, Brock. You know I didn't kill Tom."

"Knowing a thing and being able to prove it are two different things, Blue. I still have to do my job. This would all be a lot easier if you had an alibi other than your high-school-aged sister."

"Well, I don't."

"Do you have any information you can share about that day that might help?"

Blue's heart sank. She knew she had to confess, and what she was about to say wasn't going to look good. "Tom was in here earlier that day."

"Oh, okay." Brock took out his little brown leather-bound notebook and began taking notes.

Blue hated it. The whole things suddenly seemed so… official.

"He came into pick up his custom jellybean order, and he was being his usual Tom self."

"What does that mean?"

Blue sighed. "Like abrasive and condescending."

"So, you two had an altercation."

Did Brock already know?

"Why does him being a jerk mean we had an altercation?" Blue asked.

Brock stared at Blue, who shifted in her seat from one side to the other and glanced away. He could see the wheels in her head turning, the slight twitch of her lip that always gave away her apprehension. The years of conversation and eye contact had ingrained in him a deep understanding of how she worked. "Why are you answering a question with a question?" he asked. Brock could read Blue like an open book. They'd been friends forever, after all.

The best way forward was just to spill it. "Yes, there was an altercation. He was being awful, and then he just said some really terrible things about me. But it was when he brought Pepper into it."

"What could he possibly have said about Pepper?"

"He called us sluts, Brock."

"Oh, wow. That was seriously uncalled for. And all of this was over jellybeans?"'

"Yes." Blue leaned back and crossed her arms over her chest.

"Anything else?"

"I might have said something about wringing his neck. But I did say it was if I wasn't wearing heels, which I was. I'm pretty sure that means what I said doesn't meet the definition of assault."

Brock studied her. "He was strangled, Blue."

"Oh, gawd."

"Did anybody hear you say this to him?"

"Yeah, Ethan came into the shop, and right behind him were Mel and Tonya Carson."

"And they heard you threaten him?"

"Brock, I wasn't threatening him. Not really. We were just having an argument. That Tom caused!"

"Blue, you know how this looks, right? You had an altercation with the deceased in which you threatened to strangle him, and there are witnesses to that fight. I'm going to have to go talk to them right now."

"What should I do?" Blue's voice was just above a whisper.

"Don't leave town."

"Brock…" Blue choked out as he got up to leave.

Her mind raced and her heart raced faster as she looked into his eyes, searching for something – some sort of reassurance that the accusation was all a misunderstanding, a cruel joke. She wanted him to tell her that she wasn't the only suspect in this investigation, that it couldn't possibly be true. But all she saw in his eyes were doubt and worry.

"I have to go talk to them. The best way for me to help you is to let me do my job."

"Isn't that a conflict of interest? Aren't I a conflict of interest?" Blue regretted it as soon as she said it. That was twice that morning.

His lips pursed into a line. "Let me worry about my job, Blue."

Brock took off after that, and Blue was left with a sick, icky feeling in her gut. She hadn't liked the change in Brock's eyes after she told him about her argument with Tom. Blue couldn't shake the heaviness that descended after his departure, and she ran her fingers along her stomach as if she could brush away the dread that had settled there.

Her next move was to make a call she really didn't want to make. Blue and Pepper's Aunt Libby wasn't the cool aunt. At that point in their lives, she was more like an evil stepmother, if your aunt could be your evil stepmother…

Anyway.

She clutched the phone in her hand and dialed Aunt Libby's number, her knuckles turning white with the effort. Even though Aunt Libby was family, she had a sharp tongue and lofty expectations for Blue and Pepper — both of which they rarely met. The longer she waited for her aunt to answer the phone, the more her stomach clenched in dread.

The first call went to voicemail. Before she could push the button to dial Libby again, the phone rang.

"Hello, Aunt Libby," Blue said softly.

"I've been waiting all morning for you to call me, Blue. In fact, I was up half the night waiting. What's wrong with you?"

"So, I guess you've heard."

"Honey, the whole town has heard. Why didn't you call me?"

Because I didn't want to get chewed out for existing. That was the answer Blue wanted to give, but she didn't dare. "I didn't know I was a suspect until just now."

"So, you are officially a suspect? Peachy."

"I called you as soon as I found out. Brock just left the shop. You didn't answer the first call, Aunt Libby. I had the phone in my hand, finger over the dial, ready to call you again, but you beat me to it." Blue tried not to sound too annoyed.

Aunt Libby was a successful lawyer, her office downtown and her face often appearing on billboards and in newspapers. But her success was intimidating, and she was often a bit too curt. Well, curt was an understatement. Libby was downright condescending and abrasive. Blue really didn't want to talk to her, but she thought she might need Libby's advice. And advice was all she would ever get out of her aunt.

Libby wore designer clothing and drove a luxury car, but she always refused to give even the smallest portion of her wealth to her nieces. She was generous with her opinion and criticism but never with her pocketbook, and Blue couldn't help but feel a pang of bitterness each time she refused to offer anything more than words. Seeing Libby's lavish lifestyle while they struggled to buy food was difficult to ignore.

Libby's excuse was that she had to keep her finances separate from Blue's father, but Blue knew there was more to the story. She could have provided her impoverished nieces with some extra money on the sly, but instead she chose to do nothing. She could have made sure that Blue and Pepper could at least eat, but Blue knew the truth.

Aunt Libby thought she was doing Blue a favor by refusing to help. She thought that Blue should pull herself up by her bootstraps and make her own way in the world. Never mind that Libby's parents had paid for her college, all the way through law school, and the down payment on her fancy house as a graduation present. Libby had never had to pull herself up by anything.

Blue racked her brain, trying to understand why Libby was upset that she hadn't called her after Tom's death. She raised an eyebrow, surprised that Libby wanted to help. Her expression revealed her confusion. Good thing Libby couldn't see it.

"You should have called me last night." Libby sighed with her patented annoyance.

"Well, I'm calling now. I'm glad you want to help, so what should I do?" Blue asked earnestly.

"How should I know, Blue? I'm a family law attorney."

Blue just stood there blinking. "If you don't have legal advice for me, then why should I have called? I'm confused, Aunt Libby."

"You don't have to be a snot," Libby spat.

Blue bit her bottom lip. She loved being reminded why talking to Libby was a bad idea. Especially when she was already stressed. "Okay."

"Look, I'm your only family, Blue."

"Other than Pepper." Blue could no longer hide her annoyance.

"I mean your only adult family. So, you should call me when things happen in your life."

"Why, so you can condescend me and not help me at all?"

"You really are your mother's daughter."

"Aunt Libby, that's not an insult."

"You wouldn't think so. Anyway, I have to go. I have real work to do. You want some legal advice, shut up. Stop talking to Brock like he's your friend."

"He is my friend."

"He's also the undersheriff. Stop talking to him unless you have a lawyer present."

"I don't suppose you can help with that?" Blue hated to ask, but she had no idea how to hire a criminal attorney. Never in her life did she think she'd need one.

"I might know somebody. I'll need to think about it. I'll call you later." Libby hung up.

"Please don't," Blue said as she put the phone back in her purse.

Chapter Seven

Blued paced back and forth in the back of the shop, biting her nails and worrying over her predicament. She had never been in trouble with the law before and she was determined not to be this time either. Still, she was reluctant to spend money on a lawyer that she didn't have. She decided that, for now at least, she wouldn't hire one.

What she was going to do was make some money. At first, Blue had worried that the murder would hurt business.

Boy, she couldn't have been more wrong. The people of Hemlock Hollow had heard all the rumors about the murder candy lady who may have been involved in Tom's death. Curiosity and a need for sweets got the best of them, and they packed into Sucre Bleu for a glimpse of the mysterious woman and her candy. Before they left, it was hard to find one who hadn't purchased something.

At first, Blue was taken aback by the constant sound of the cash register and annoyed by the hustle and bustle of customers craning their necks to get a good look at her. But soon she was counting up her earnings with a satisfied grin on her face.

Pepper arrived after her half-day at school and stood in awe at the door to the candy store, astounded by the sea of bodies that had gathered in the short few hours since she left that morning.

"You should kill someone more often," Pepper joked.

Blue shot her a look. "Just for that, you can get to work."

"Do I get paid?" Pepper asked, but even as she did, she slipped on a pair of gloves to help box up orders.

"Don't mess with me, Pepper. Haven't you heard the rumors?"

The sound of Pepper's laughter rang through the store as she and her sister worked in tandem. Moving quickly and efficiently, they filled orders with boxes of colorful candy. As the last customer left, Pepper gave her sister a quick hug before making her way to the back room. She needed a break and to use the restroom before grabbing a granola bar Blue had stashed in her purse.

After filling a couple more orders, an unexpected customer stepped up to the counter. Blue swallowed hard as she studied the woman's face.

"Margery… uh, how can I help you?"

"What did he buy yesterday?" she demanded.

"I'm sorry, what?"

"What did Tom buy yesterday? I know he was here, the police told me. So, out with it? What did he buy?"

Blue thought it over. It wasn't like she was a lawyer or therapist, so there wasn't any reason she couldn't tell Margery about Tom's order, right?

"It was a custom jellybean order. He wanted jellybeans that taste like blackberries and lavender."

"I knew it," she snarled. "I just knew it."

"I'm sorry, I don't understand." Because Blue thought that the order was a gift for his wife. Maybe his mother or an aunt or something, but she had no idea why Margery would be upset about jellybeans.

"They were for that little trollop. He told me that he would never betray me, but he was a lying snake."

"I'm sorry." Blue didn't know what else to say.

Margery let out a long exhale, and her shoulders slumped. "I should be sadder."

"I…" Blue stuttered.

"I'm glad he's gone. There I said it. I'm better off without him."

Blue stared at Margery, not sure how to respond. Margery's face was filled with anguish as she tapped a finger to her lips, her eyes welling with tears. She let out a strangled sob, spun on her heel, and sprinted out of the candy shop and into the town square.

"You look like you need this," Pepper said and offered Blue a tray of chocolate and pecan turtles.

"Did you make these?" Blue asked and plucked one off the tray.

"You had everything in the back ready to go," Pepper responded.

"But how? We've been so busy?" She popped the turtle in her mouth and chewed it up. Even she had to admit that it was really, really good.

"Little touch of magic makes everything easier." Pepper's smile spread across her entire face. She lit up.

"Pepper."

"Oh, come on, sis. You said we could. Maybe this will help out our profit margins a little bit."

Blue was about to argue, but her vision swam. Her knees went weak just before everything went black.

When she came to, Ethan was hovering over her. Concern etched his features, and she felt his warm, strong hand enveloping hers.

"I knew you were too good to be true." Blue's voice was barely above a whisper.

"Come again?" Ethan responded.

"I knew you were a dream. You're too beautiful to be real."

"Is she awake?" Pepper came running into the room with a glass of water.

It was then Blue realized she wasn't dreaming. And she'd really said what she just said to Ethan.

"Yeah, she's awake." Ethan squeezed Blue's hand. "Are you okay?"

Blue looked over at Pepper, who quickly looked away. "What happened?"

Pepper didn't say anything. She still wouldn't look at Blue. That's when Blue knew her sister had put something in the candy. Probably to make her relax. The name 'tranquility turtles' floated through her mind. The magic had worked too well.

"I'm going to give you ladies a ride home." Ethan helped Blue sit up. "All I've got is the bike, though. So, we'll have to take your car."

"I can drive," Pepper offered. "I can drive us home, so you don't have to go to the trouble."

"She doesn't have a license," Blue said it before Ethan could agree. "But I can drive. I'm fine."

"You're not, Blue. I'll drive the two of you home. I promise I'll be careful with your car."

"But what about your bike?"

"I'll walk back to my office after I drop you guys off."

"That's at least a mile. Maybe two." Blue didn't know for sure. She'd never mapped it out.

"I'll be fine."

Ethan reached out to Blue, his hand hovering in the air, unsure of what he was allowed to do. She smiled weakly and nodded to signal that it was okay. He carefully helped to stand, propping her up with his arm under her shoulders and around her back. She swayed precariously and would have collapsed if he hadn't been there to support her. He contemplated picking her up and carrying her, but in the end chose to keep his arm around her waist, steadying her as she stumbled one foot in front of the other toward the entrance of the shop. He kept up his slow and steady pace, not breaking until they reached the doors. Ethan supported her, and she moved her feet across the sidewalk, and as long as that was working, he'd keep going.

As Ethan assisted Blue into the car, Pepper shuffled around the shop, double-checking that the doors and windows were secured. Once satisfied, she locked the shop's front door and headed to the car. Pepper handed Ethan Blue's keys with a smile.

Blue opened the passenger-side car door and slid into the seat, leaving Pepper standing outside. She glanced up at Ethan hopefully, as if willing him to invite her to take the wheel. But he said nothing, and after a few moments of hesitation, Pepper reluctantly climbed into the backseat.

"This is quite the car," Ethan said as he put the key in the ignition and turned it over.

"It was my Gran's," Blue said and patted the door.

Her heart dropped when she realized the protection sigil was still carved into the dust on the driver's side. But if Ethan noticed, he didn't say anything. Besides, even if he did, he'd probably think it was just a doodle anyway.

"What year is it?" Ethan asked as he pulled the long, red Cadillac away from the curb.

"2003. But it really was Gran's Sunday driver."

"I can tell. Under fifty thousand miles. If you take good care of this baby, it'll be a classic someday."

"Someday," Blue agreed.

"So, it's got the big eight in it?"

"I assume you mean the eight-cylinder engine?"

"That I do," Ethan agreed.

"Yes. It's kind of a beastie."

"You're better off with the eight cylinders. The sixes from that era weren't nearly as good. It uses more gas, but this car will last you a long time."

"You know a lot about cars?" Blue asked.

"Yeah, I thought you were a biker or something." Pepper didn't look up from her phone to make the snarky comment.

"I know enough to get by," he said with a shrug.

The car buzzed with an uncomfortable silence until they finally pulled into the driveway. As soon as the car stopped, Pepper leapt out and rushed to unlock the front door. Inside, she scampered up the stairs, calling out a warning to Tiffany that they had guests.

Ethan carefully assisted Blue out of the car and up the porch steps, propping her up with one arm to keep her steady. His other hand reached for the doorknob as he asked, "Should I be taking you to a hospital? Pepper said you didn't eat today, and your blood sugar dropped, but is that all that's happening?" He was met with momentary silence.

"I was wondering why you were there when I woke up…" Blue said it more to herself than to Ethan.

"I thought maybe it was because I was your guardian angel or something." Ethan smiled impishly.

Blue's face flushed a deep scarlet as she clutched her forehead and stammered, "I-I-I didn't say that, did I? Please tell me I didn't say that."

"You did not, but you did say that I was a dream come true."

"I did not." Blue hid her face in her hands.

"You didn't, but it was something along those lines."

"Can we just forget I said that? I wasn't feeling well."

"So, you don't think I'm good-looking?" Ethan deadpanned.

"Not when you're fishing for compliments."

"Ouch. Wow."

"I'm totally kidding, and yes, you are quite handsome. But you already knew that."

"Well, that's an especially nice comment coming from someone like you."

"Someone like me?" Blue asked.

"Oh, come on… You said that I know that I'm handsome. Surely, you know you're beautiful, Blue. Strikingly so."

"Are you flirting with me?"

"I think I am," Ethan said with a nervous chuckle. "And perhaps I should go. I'd hate to do something… stupid."

"Stupid?"

"Unwanted. You seem like you're feeling better, but I imagine you need rest. I don't want to take advantage."

Blue muttered "A true gentleman" under her breath, and she dared to lift her gaze to meet his. His eyes were like deep blue pools that held her captive, and she felt a cool shiver of electricity course through her veins. She couldn't break away from the intensity of their connection and had the urge to reach out and touch his face, an urge she quickly squashed lest she do something rash like kiss him. "Thank you for making sure I got home and safely to the sofa. I think I'm going to get a glass of water, though."

The effort of standing up was too much for Blue. She felt the room spin, her legs wobble beneath her, and her stomach tighten. She lurched back onto the sofa, her head spinning, and pressed her forehead into the palms of her hands.

"Whoa," Ethan said. He rubbed slow circles on her back. "Breathe in through your nose and out through your mouth. Slowly."

Blue listened, but she also thought about how she wanted to strangle Pepper. But after a few deep breaths, she realized her sister hadn't meant any harm, and if she'd encouraged her to practice magic properly at an early age, none of this would be happening.

"Let me get you a glass of water." Ethan squeezed her hand and started off out of the living room. "Which way to the kitchen?"

"I've got it!" Pepper called out from the kitchen.

She'd been hiding in her room but had the door open. So, she heard her sister nearly pass out again.

Ethan sank into the well-worn cushions of the sofa and waited. Pepper emerged from down the hall, her steps quick and purposeful. She had a sweating glass of water in one hand and a bottle of chilled Coke in the other.

Blue looked up at her sister. "The Coke, please," she said, and Pepper handed it over. "Leave the water too, though."

"I'm so sorry," Pepper said.

"For what?" Ethan seemed perplexed. It was the second time Pepper had apologized.

"I accidentally took her lunch to school with me," Pepper lied quickly. "It's my fault her blood sugar crashed so hard."

Blue wasn't sure whether she should be worried or impressed.

"Oh, okay," Ethan said.

"And she always forgets to eat anyway," Pepper continued. "Without her lunch, I'm sure she didn't eat anything today."

Ethan's gaze lingered on Blue for a moment too long. Her throat was dry, her pulse raced, and her stomach was filled with dread. She had to stick to their story, no matter how much she wanted to tell him the truth. She slowly nodded her head, hoping he didn't notice the slight tremble in her chin. She couldn't bear the thought of him thinking she was nuts. It would be worse if he actually knew the truth.

"I'm genuinely worried that this is more than just a missed meal, you guys. I feel bad leaving you alone. Especially if you won't go to the ER."

"I'm here, she'll be fine." Pepper swallowed nervously.

"No offense, kid, but you're a kid."

"What are you trying to say?" Blue asked.

"Maybe I should stay. I think you need someone here to keep an eye on you. An adult."

"Oh, it's really not that bad." Blue tried to smile reassuringly.

"I don't think you realize how sick you look right now, Blue." The concern etched deeper on Ethan's face.

"Wow, thanks." Blue frowned. But she also realized that if she didn't let Ethan stay, she might need to call Aunt Libby to babysit her. That thought turned her stomach. There would be no end to Libby's criticisms.

"I don't mean it like that. I just… Hey, if you don't want me in the house, I totally get that. Two young women alone, and a guy like me asks to stay. Yeah, I get that's a lot. Especially since I'm new in town. But I can walk back and get my bike. And then I'll sleep in your car in the driveway after I check in on you again."

"Why would you do that?" Blue asked.

"Because I'm worried about you. And I want to be here if you need me. I can sleep in the driveway or in the garage, and then if you need me in the middle of the night, I'm just a hop, skip, and a jump away."

Blue watched Ethan Moore carefully. His expression was calm and open, and his body language was relaxed. He met her gaze with honest eyes that were wide with genuine concern. She could feel the intensity of his protective energy without him saying a single word.

"You can stay on the sofa," Blue decided.

"Blue…" Pepper protested.

Blue looked up at Pepper, who had her lips pursed in thought. The tiny lines around her eyes and mouth told Blue that, while Pepper was still concerned, she wasn't too worried about Ethan. After all, she had trusted him enough to go get him when Blue had passed out, and she was a witch too. She could sense danger, so if she felt that Ethan presented no threat, then he didn't. Pepper ultimately shrugged and headed off to her room.

After she drank her Coke, Blue was finally able to stand. Ethan stayed right at her side, but she was able to go to the hall closet and get a blanket, sheets and a pillow for him.

She tried to make up the sofa for him, but Ethan insisted he could do it himself. He walked her to the bathroom door, but when Blue shot him a look, Ethan threw up his hands in surrender and retreated to the living room.

Once Blue had tucked herself into bed, she heard Ethan in the bathroom. After a few minutes, she heard him leave the bathroom and go back to the living room.

She lay there for a long time wondering if he was comfortable or if she was being an idiot letting what was essentially a strange man stay in her house.

After a half hour, Blue got up and made her way down to Pepper's room. She knocked on the door, and when Pepper answered, she slipped inside.

"I'm staying in here with you tonight," Blue said as she locked Pepper's bedroom door.

"You're the one who told him he could stay here tonight," Pepper said with an eyeroll. "If you're worried he's a serial killer, then kick him out."

"I don't," Blue said resolutely. "But you're my sister, and I'm staying in here tonight just to be sure."

"Fine, but I get the left side of the bed," Pepper decided.

"It's your bed."

Blue slipped between the soft, cool sheets and sighed in contentment. She could feel Pepper's magical power still coursing through her veins, lulling her into a deep, restorative sleep. But she was too weary to fight it, so she let her dreams take her. She didn't rouse when Pepper got back up out of the bed.

Pepper slowly turned the doorknob and opened the door to her bedroom, just enough to peek out. She tiptoed to the living room, where Ethan lay on the sofa, his chest rising and falling in time with his deep, rhythmic snores.

Convinced the coast was clear, and that her sister was safe, she went back to her bedroom and locked the door again. After that, Pepper quietly opened her bedroom window and slipped out into the night.

Chapter Eight

Blue stirred from her deep sleep and when her blurred vision focused, the sight of Tiffany's head looming mere inches above hers was unmistakable. Her cold, wet nose glided up Blue's cheek as Tiffany dug her claws into her collarbone. Tiffany's eyes gleamed with life.

"There's a man on the sofa. I killed him," Tiffany said.

Blue shot straight up and accidently knocked Tiffany to the floor. "You didn't!"

Pepper stirred in the darkness, feeling the mattress dip ever so slightly as she rolled over to face the window. Through the cracks of the curtains, the first hints of morning light were seeping through. She had been careful to sneak back in, tiptoeing across the room and silently slipping into bed beside Blue, who was unaware of her late-night escapade.

"Hey," Tiffany protested. "Don't have a cow. I'm just kidding."

Blue shot Tiffany a look and stepped out into the hallway and onto the landing. She glanced down, half expecting to see Ethan lying there peacefully, but he wasn't. All that remained was a neatly folded pile of blankets on the sofa. On top was a note from Ethan explaining why he had left.

Blue read over the note with mixed emotions. Part of her felt relieved that she had woken up to find him gone, yet another part of her felt disappointed that he hadn't stayed to say goodbye properly.

Blue, I'm sorry I had to leave so early. I had a personal obligation I had to see too. Since you hadn't had any kind of emergency in the night, I figured you were feeling much better. Plus, I noticed that you were sleeping in your sister's room. I hope that I did not make the two of you too uncomfortable. Please call me if you need me for anything. -Ethan.

A sense of admiration overwhelmed her as she stared at the blankets, neatly folded and stacked on Ethan's makeshift bed. He had taken such care in arranging them. It seemed like something more than just courtesy. The gesture showed an appreciation for Blue's home and hospitality. She was even more certain of her assessment that Ethan was a good man.

Blue sighed softly as she picked up the bedding and tucked it back into the hall closet. As she walked back upstairs Pepper's bedroom, Tiffany purred contentedly while rubbing against Blue's ankles in appreciation.

Pepper groggily climbed out of bed and rubbed her eyes, still not quite sure what was happening. But as soon as Blue mentioned breakfast, an eager smile lit up her face.

"Omelets?" she asked hopefully.

"I suppose we do have the ingredients."

Blue nodded and the two of them headed to the kitchen. Blue cracked eggs into a bowl while Pepper chopped up onions, mushrooms and peppers for their omelets. The two sisters chatted about the night's events as they cooked, wondering why Ethan had left so early but grateful that he had not turned out to be a serial killer.

When their omelets were done, Blue poured two cups of coffee and they sat down to enjoy a delicious breakfast together in peace and quiet.

But it wouldn't last. As soon as they were halfway through their breakfast, Blue brought up the tranquility turtles from the day before.

"We need to talk about your use of magic."

"Blue, I really didn't mean to do that."

"I know you didn't, but I hope you understand that you shouldn't have given me magic candies without telling me."

Pepper sighed, "I know. I'm sorry. But it was all so exciting and new. I just wanted to do something special for you."

Blue softened a bit as she listened to Pepper's sincere apology. She reached out and grabbed her hand, offering an understanding smile.

"Magic can be dangerous," Blue warned gently. "You have to be careful when using it and make sure you understand the consequences of your actions."

She went on to explain that magic could lead to unpredictable outcomes, not only for those using the magic but also for those around them who may be affected by its use. She reminded Pepper that with great power comes great responsibility, and that she must always think carefully before using her magic in order to avoid any unintended consequences.

"Does that mean we can't make magic candies for the shop?" the teen asked sincerely.

"Pepper," Blue warned.

"Oh, come on. We could make so much money. I know we can't tell people there's magic in the candy, but people would flock to buy our treats if they... I don't know... gave them a boost or helped them relax."

"I can't believe you'd ask that after what happened to me," Blue responded.

"But you could help me. It's true that I made them too powerful, but you could help me. We could perfect the recipes."

"I'm not doing that just to make money," Blue said.

"But we could help people too."

That stopped Blue in her tracks. Most of the time, she treated their witchcraft like it was a disease to be avoided, but shouldn't they be using their gifts to help others? Didn't they have some sort of karmic obligation to do so?

"We'll talk about it later."

Pepper looked as if she was about to complain, but she just offered her older sister a tight nod. "I'll take that as a yes."

That made Blue laugh. After that, Pepper headed off to school, and Blue made her way to the candy shop.

She almost expected to see Ethan there waiting for her, but once again, he wasn't around. His note had said he had some personal business to attend to, so Blue assumed he was still attending to it.

But as Blue surveyed the shelves of candy, she was reminded of the previous conversation with Pepper. Was it really possible to make magic candies with beneficial effects? All she knew for certain is that she wasn't going to trust any recipes from Pepper.

Blue decided it was time to take matters into her own hands and put her creative mind to work. She began brainstorming ideas for possible magical candy recipes, conjuring up images of sweet and tasty treats that could provide benefits such as increased energy, improved focus or a calming boost.

Some ideas included sugar cookie fudge with a sprinkle of fairy dust on top, chewy gummy bears infused with mint leaves for an invigorating jolt of energy, chocolate truffles containing a blend of herbs known to reduce anxiety and stress, sticky honey drops made with roses petals and lavender buds for relaxation, or crunchy nut clusters mixed with dried rosemary that would help improve concentration.

The possibilities seemed endless, and none of those ideas technically required actual magic. She could make the treats and advertise them and new herbal candies, and if she felt comfortable, add just a pinch of magic to accentuate the herbs' effects.

Blue felt most eager to make the nut clusters with rosemary. She'd make a sweet syrup infused with the herb to help the mixed nuts stick together.

She'd need a few things, and while she'd normally order them from her supplier, Blue was in a hurry to make the candies right away. The store was supposed to be open, but she didn't have any customers. Blue figured it wouldn't hurt to close the shop for a few minutes and pop over to the general store across the square.

So, she went to the store and grabbed all the ingredients she'd need for her recipes. She bought sugar, butter, chocolate chips, dried herbs, fresh herbs, roses to use their petals, dried mint leaves and a variety of nuts. Blue had intended to begin with the rosemary nut clusters, but she was so excited she bought everything she needed to make all of her ideas.

A few minutes later, she had checked out at the store. Blue hurried back across the square and into Sucre Bleu. She turned the sign back to "Open," but since there still weren't any customers, she headed back to the kitchen again.

She was so excited to get started that she gathered some glass jars from the shop to store all her ingredients in until she was ready to use them. She assembled a workstation with baking trays and bowls at one end of the store where she could mix her magical ingredients by hand before adding them to the recipes. Once her supplies were organized, Blue couldn't wait to get started on creating some wonderful new treats that could help others have a better day.

First, she began with the nut clusters. She heated a pan on the stove and added some butter and sugar to make a simple but rich syrup. As the mix melted together, Blue stirred in some rosemary so that its subtle flavor could infuse into the liquid. When it was done, Blue poured the tasty syrup over her selection of nuts and gave them a good stir until all of them were evenly coated. Once she was sure that each cluster had enough syrup to hold them together, Blue spooned them onto parchment paper-lined baking trays before transferring them to an oven heated to 350°F.

After about ten minutes in the hot oven, Blue opened it up to find a golden brown tray of delicious-smelling nut clusters. She couldn't wait to try one. After they cooled down, Blue removed them from the tray and put them in jars so they would stay fresh longer. Finally satisfied with her work, she set out crafting her other candies.

Next up were the chocolate truffles, which called for a bit more finesse than the nut clusters but were still relatively easy to make. To start, Blue melted some bittersweet chocolate chips in a double boiler before stirring in a mixture of dried lavender and chamomile flowers. She let the mix cool down before adding some cream and rolling it into small balls that she placed on parchment paper-lined baking sheets. Blue put those into the walk-in to cool down completely.

When they were hardened, Blue removed them from the fridge and rolled each truffle into a small ball with her hands before dusting them with powdered sugar for an extra sweet finish. Then she rolled each one in cocoa powder for an even more extra special touch. She considered sprinkling them with fairy dust but decided against it. Blue hadn't worked with fairy dust in a long time, and the last thing she wanted to do was go overboard. Pepper had done that, and it hadn't ended well. Blue did not want customers passing out in the shop. Or worse…

Finally, she transferred all of her finished treats into beautiful glass jars so that her customers could choose whichever one suited their needs best.

She was about to get started on the gummy bears when the bells over the door jingled. She had a customer.

Blue looked up to see a tall, lanky figure standing in the doorway. He was wearing a heavy trench coat and sunglasses, despite the fact it was now raining outside. The man didn't say anything, he simply stood there and looked around for a moment before he turned his gaze back towards Blue.

"Welcome!" Blue said with a friendly smile. "Can I help you find something?"

The man nodded slowly but didn't move or speak. Blue couldn't help but notice that he seemed on edge and fidgety, as if he was expecting something bad to happen at any second. His behavior made her suspect that maybe he was up to no good. But perhaps he was just a looky-loo who'd come to the shop because of Tom's murder. The day before, there had been dozens of people who just showed up to get a look at the murder candy lady. Apparently, they'd all found a new distraction. Except for this particular man who was making her a little uncomfortable.

She cleared her throat nervously and asked him again what kind of candy he was looking for today.

"I have an internet order," he said softly.

Blue realized she was being judgmental. Perhaps he was wearing the sunglasses because he got migraines. Maybe he was just shy and from the next town over. People sometimes drove to Hemlock Hollow just to get her candies.

"Sure," she said with a smile. "What's the name on the order?"

Suddenly, the tall, lanky man spoke up. "I'm Detective Jameson," he said. "I'm here to investigate Tom's murder. Do you mind answering a few questions?" Blue eyed him suspiciously. She didn't recognize him.

"What kind of detective?" she asked cautiously, her heart beginning to thump in her chest. "Because you just said you had an internet order."

He asked her in a gruff voice, "Have you seen anything suspicious in the past couple of days? Any new faces around town?"

She shook her head. "No, I haven't seen anything."

"Are you sure?" He peered at her intently, like he was trying to read her mind. "Think hard, Blue. I need answers."

She clenched her jaw. "I already told you, I haven't seen anything."

But that wasn't true. Not only did she get in an altercation with Tom, but there was a new face in town. Ethan had moved in next door. But wouldn't the detective already know that?

"Margery Wiseman was in here after the murder demanding to know what kind of candy Tom had purchased before he died. She was upset. I think Tom might have been having an affair," Blue offered because she figured that was better than throwing herself or Ethan under the bus to appease this strange man.

He shook his head. "No, I don't think that's it."

"Excuse me?" Blue asked.

Detective Jameson sighed and pushed his sunglasses up on his head. "I don't think Tom was having an affair," he said, "although that would be a much simpler explanation. Margery Wiseman had her suspicions, but I think we are looking at something far more sinister here."

Blue couldn't believe what she was hearing. She had assumed that Tom's death was a result of infidelity or the result of a crime of passion. But it seemed Detective Jameson believed there was something else going on in this town, something dark and sinister.

"What makes you so sure it wasn't an affair?" Blue asked curiously. "Do you have any evidence to back up your claim?"

She expected some kind of justification for his beliefs, but instead he simply nodded and smiled cryptically. He hadn't answered her question directly, but it seemed as though he wanted her to figure out the answer for herself. Or he was just a weirdo.

"If it wasn't an affair then what's your theory?" Blue asked despite secretly wishing the strange man would turn around and leave her shop immediately.

Detective Jameson took a deep breath and looked around the room. He seemed to be taking in the details of the shop, from Blue's friendly smile to the colorful array of candies displayed on her shelves. He had been observing her silently for several minutes, almost as if he was trying to figure out something about her.

Finally, he cleared his throat and spoke. "I'm not at liberty to discuss my theories publicly," he said with a hint of smugness in his voice. "But I can assure you that I'm here for a reason and I'm the one asking all the questions."

"Well, there's nothing I can tell you that I haven't already told you or the sheriff's department."

At the mention of the sheriff's Department, the man's eyes darkened. "Thank you for your time," he said and spun on his heels. Within seconds, he had hurried out of the shop.

On instinct, Blue rushed to the window. She watched the man walk down the street and get into a black sedan parked nearby. The car had tinted windows and a gleaming exterior, suggesting it was an expensive model. Without warning, the car started to move, and he drove away from Blue's candy shop at a rapid speed.

Blue stood there for a moment, still in shock from the conversation she just had with Detective Jameson. What did he mean by his comments? What was he trying to find out and why was he so cryptic about it? A million different thoughts raced through her mind and she suddenly had a strong urge to call Brock and tell him immediately what had just happened.

She quickly pulled her phone out of her pocket and started dialing Brock's number when she heard another car engine roar in the distance. Blue glanced outside again and saw another black sedan coming down the street, this one obviously not as expensive or sleek as the first one. The man who got out of the vehicle looked suspiciously similar to Detective Jameson. The man was same height and build, but when he turned to face her direction, Blue saw it was a completely different person. He took a few steps and disappeared into the salon.

Okay, she thought, *so I'm not living in that kind of horror movie.* At that point, she went to the back and got her phone. After scrolling through her contacts, she found Brock and hit "call."

Aunt Libby's words rang through her head as she waited for Brock to answer. Libby had told her to stop talking to Brock, but Libby had also said she'd call Blue back with some sort of advice. And she hadn't, so *screw Aunt Libby,* Blue thought.

"Hello, Blue," Brock said when he answered.

"Hey, Brock," she said quickly. "Something strange just happened at my shop. I think you should know about it."

"What is it?" Brock asked with a hint of curiosity in his voice.

Blue told him about Detective Jameson and the car that drove away shortly after their conversation. She also mentioned the second car but left out the fact that the man in it resembled Detective Jameson.

When she finished, there was a short pause and then Brock spoke again. "I don't know anyone by the name of Detective Jameson working for our department," he said sternly. "Are you sure he's from around here?"

"I did not recognize him. He flashed a badge, but I didn't look close enough at it. I wish I had."

Brock sighed and then went silent for a few moments before speaking again. "Listen, Blue, I want you to be careful and keep an eye out for anything suspicious in your shop. I'll ask around and see if there is another jurisdiction interested in Tom's case, but I assume they would have reached out to me before they started interviewing witnesses."

"Okay," Blue said, feeling a bit better knowing that Brock was going to look into it.

"In the meantime, I want you to be extra careful and if you see or hear anything out of the ordinary, don't hesitate to call me," he added. "We'll figure this out."

Blue thanked him and they hung up a few moments later. She took a deep breath and got back to work on her new candies.

Everything seemed quiet now and she had almost forgotten about Detective Jameson when something caught her eye on the counter. It was a small note with her name written on it in scrawled handwriting. She quickly opened it up and read the words written inside: Meet me tonight at The Rusty Nail at 8:00 sharp.

Blue's heart raced as she quickly folded up the note and stuffed it into her pocket. What was this all about? Was Detective Jameson behind this? Or someone else? Whatever it was, Blue knew she had to find out.

"Hey, Blue, how are you feeling today?" Ethan asked as he walked into the shop.

"I'm much better than yesterday, thanks for asking," Blue replied. She hesitated for a moment, considering asking him about the personal business that had made him leave without saying goodbye that morning. But she decided not to pry. Instead, she pulled out a mysterious note. "I could use your help with something."

Blue reached into her pocket and pulled out a crumpled piece of paper. "I found this note and I'm trying to figure out what it means. Would you mind checking it out with me?"

Ethan took the note from her and smoothed it out. "What do you think it's about?"

"Well, earlier today a man came in pretending to be a detective investigating Tom's death. Detective Jameson, he said. I think he left this note," Blue explained. "Though I have no idea why."

Ethan raised an eyebrow. "That's strange. Do you think this Detective Jameson left the note?"

Blue nodded. "I'm almost certain of it. No one else came into the shop between our conversation and me finding the note. I think he might be trying to lead me to something, or maybe he's trying to set me up for something. I'm not sure. That's why I want to go check out this place called The Rusty Nail tonight. Maybe we'll find some clues there."

Ethan looked up from the note. "Are you asking me to come with you?"

Blue nodded. "If you're not busy, I could use some backup. And besides, you're always up for an adventure, right?"

Ethan chuckled. "That's true. I'm in. What time should we meet?"

"I need to be there at 8:00 according to the note, so we should meet by 7:30."

"Should I pick you up?" Ethan asked.

"I'd rather take a car than a motorcycle, sorry. I'll pick you up."

Ethan asked, "Is this a date?"

Blue hesitated, a furtive smile crossing her lips. "No, it's not. I just thought I would be safer with a little backup."

Ethan nodded. "Okay, no date. I'll see you at 7:30 tonight."

Just as Ethan left the shop, and before Blue could evaluate the tone in his voice, a young woman walked in and began browsing the selection of caramels. She seemed to be muttering under her breath about something. Blue couldn't help but overhear her say, "If it was you who killed that Tom guy, then good for you! He had it coming after what he did to me."

Blue gasped in shock and stepped forward. "What do you mean? What did Tom do to you?"

The woman's face contorted in rage as she spoke, her cheeks now the same color as her flowing red locks. She recounted the horror of that night when Tom had carelessly swerved and crashed into their car, only to immediately take off without leaving a trace. They were now left with an astronomical repair bill that they had no way of paying.

"I had days where I couldn't afford to eat. Sometimes I got so hungry that I almost went dumpster diving. My power got cut off a couple of times, and I almost got evicted. The worst part is that slimy jerk actually came around and said he'd help me out financially if I slept with him. I refused, of course, but it made my life so hard. Plus, he was so creepy, I was actually kind of afraid of him sometimes."

Tears threatened to tumble over as she finished her story, and Blue felt nothing but sympathy for the woman's plight. But was there more to the story? Did the pretty young woman really want him to die over a car crash?

"How do you know for sure it was Tom?" Blue asked cautiously.

The woman paused, her gaze shifting away from Blue and towards the floor. She then looked up with a determined expression on her face and said, "Because I saw him with my own eyes that night. Even though it was dark out, there was no mistaking his sneering face. I'm Kimber, by the way. You can check. I live down the street from Tom's... from where Tom lived."

Blue's brows were furrowed in concentration as she packed a variety of caramels and handed Kimber a small, colorful cardboard box containing the candies. Kimber's eyes lit up, and she accepted the box with a warm smile.

"You don't have to do this," she said. "I'm doing better financially now. It was rough, but I'm doing better. I wasn't fishing for freebies."

"I know," Blue said. "But take them. Please. It will make me happy."

Kimber took the box and tucked it into her huge pink leather purse. "Thank you so much."

"You're welcome, Kimber. There is one little thing you can do for me, though."

"What's that?"

"Can you think of anyone else who might have had a reason to kill Tom? Did your other neighbors hate him as much?"

"Oh, everyone hated him," Kimber said with a chuckle. "Uh... But the person on our block who hated him the most, even more than me, was Jack Malone."

"Why did Jack hate Tom so much?"

"Tom harassed Jack almost nonstop, but he was good at it. He did it in a way that Jack could never get the police to do anything about it."

"Any idea why Tom was bothering him?"

"From what I understand, Tom thought Jack was up to something... or he thought he was some sort of criminal. So, he was always looking for evidence," Kimber said, and she made air quotes around the word "evidence."

"That's... weird. And Brock... I mean Undersheriff McKinley, couldn't do anything about it?"

"Just like with me and the car crash, we could never get enough evidence. Tom was just too slippery. The way I see it, the only way Jack could get Tom to leave him alone was to kill him."

"I see."

"Hey, I've got to go. I've got to take my mom to the doctor. Thank you so much for the caramels. It means a lot to me."

"You're most welcome."

"I'll come back soon and buy something next time. Or if I think of anything about Tom, I'll drop in."

Blue nodded and watched as Kimber walked away, her red hair shimmering in the sunlight. As she disappeared down the street, Blue thought about what Kimber had said. Could Jack have really been capable of murder? It seemed like a stretch, but then again, stranger things had happened before. She didn't know Jack at all, but it seemed like a weak motive for murder.

Blue decided to pay Jack a visit later that day to get more information. She figured it would be worth it in order to get the full story about Tom and find out if he was truly behind his death. After all, she was determined to get justice for everyone who had suffered from Tom's cruel behavior.

Serendipity struck later that afternoon when Pepper texted Blue to say she was studying and having dinner with a friend after school. That meant once Blue closed the candy shop for the day, she'd have time to drop by Jack's house before she had to meet Ethan to go to The Rusty Nail.

Blue knew Tom's neighborhood, but she didn't know Jack's specific address. She tried Googling it, but the actual location was behind one of those "find anybody" paywalls. So, even though she'd just seen Ethan, she walked next door.

His bike was out front, and the lights were on, so Blue went inside. She took in the high ceilings, exposed brick walls, and large windows that let in plenty of natural light. The main room was spacious, with a desk in the center and a comfortable couch and armchair off to the side. There were a few plants on the windowsills, and the hardwood floors are polished to a shine. The desk was orderly, with a computer, a lamp, and a few framed photos on top. When Blue walked around to the side of the desk, she saw that the photo frames were empty. They were just for show, and Blue assumed that most clients didn't go behind Ethan's desk.

There were filing cabinets and storage shelves along the walls, and everything was labeled and organized. She could see a small kitchenette in the back of the office, with a new mini fridge, a microwave, and a coffee maker.

"Can I help you?" Ethan asked as he emerged from a room off the kitchenette.

"Where'd you get plants?" Blue asked. "Did you bring these from your old office?"

"They were on sale at the hardware store," Ethan admitted sheepishly. "I did bring the old ones from my former office, but they died before I could move them from my house into the office."

"Interesting."

"Is that why you're here? You want some plant suggestions for your shop? I'm probably not your guy," Ethan laughed.

"I'm actually here because I want to use you," Blue deadpanned.

"Excuse me?" Ethan asked and his cheeks turned a furious shade of red.

It made Blue chuckle. "I need an address and I don't want to pay for it. I figured you had a source for such things."

"Oh," Ethan said and tugged at his collar. "Right. Yeah, so I usually charge for skip tracing, but I guess for you, I can offer a coupon."

"A coupon?" Blue laughed again. "It's a local address. I know the street; I just need a house number."

"I suppose," Ethan teased. "But you only get one freebie. Next time you have to hire me just like everyone else."

Blue rolled her eyes playfully. "Next time I'll just pay for the lookup on FindAnyone.com."

"You wound me, Blue."

"Yeah, yeah. Save your complaints for when we go out later. For now, about that address."

Ethan nodded and sat down at his desk. Blue gave him Jack's name and what street he lived on, and within seconds, Ethan had a house number.

"I'd ask what you're doing, but I figure if you wanted me to know, you'd tell me."

"Just looking into one of Tom's neighbors. It's not dangerous or anything, but if you want to come along, you're welcome," Blue offered.

Ethan's eyes darted to the clock. "I wish I could. But if we're going to meet at 7:30, I've got a couple of things I have to do first."

"Well, then I'll get out of your hair. Thanks for the address."

"See you later, Blue."

"Later, Ethan."

***

When Blue arrived at Jack's house, she found him pacing back and forth in his living room, wringing his hands together anxiously. She could see him clearly through the giant plate glass window on the front of the house.

He looked up when he heard her knock on the door and noticed that he was being watched. He instantly stopped pacing and cleared his throat before speaking up in a shaky voice: "What do you want?"

Blue could tell immediately that something was wrong, and she asked Jack if she could come in. "I'm here to talk to you," she said. "Can I come in?"

Jack studied her for a moment through the window. "Who are you?"

"I'm Blue Bell. I own Sucre Bleu down at the square. I'm here to talk to you about Tom. I'm here to help, I promise."

He studied her for another moment and then seemed to make a decision. Jack came to the front door and opened it. He stepped back and let Blue into the small, cluttered entryway. As soon as she was in, he slammed the door and locked the deadbolt and the knob.

"I'm being watched," he said, gesturing towards the window. "I don't know who it is, but I've seen someone lurking around my house for a few days now."

Blue looked out the window but didn't see anyone. She asked Jack to describe the person he saw and where they might be hiding.

Jack pointed to a cluster of bushes across the street from his house. "The person I saw seemed to be hiding in those bushes over there," he said.

Blue stepped outside, walked over to the bushes, and carefully parted them with her hands. To her surprise, she discovered a small camera nestled among the leaves and branches pointing directly at Jack's house.

Blue examined it carefully before motioning for Jack to come out of his house. She showed him where she found the camera and then removed it from its mount. Together, they took it back inside so they could try to figure out why someone would be spying on Jack.

They looked at the footage from the camera to see if they could find any clues as to who placed it there. The footage showed a few different people, some of them familiar and some not. One person in particular seemed to be keeping an eye on Jack's house, but their identity was obscured by a hat and sunglasses.

Blue and Jack continued to watch the footage, but they couldn't make out any faces or identities.

Eventually, they had to turn off the footage.

"Jack, who do you think has been watching you?" Blue's voice was calm, but her eyes betrayed a flicker of concern as she watched him closely.

Jack's reply came in a cascade of names, each more obscure than the last. Blue's expression shifted subtly, a crease forming between her brows as she weighed the reality of his words.

"I need to head out," she said, her tone gentle yet firm. "But I'll look into this, Jack. Whoever left that camera, whoever's doing this, I'll help you figure it out."

Jack's gaze, clouded with unease, followed her. "What should I do in the meantime?" he asked, his voice laced with a quiet desperation.

Blue paused, considering her words carefully. "Try not to worry too much. Maybe add some extra security around your house? Motion-sensitive lights, a security system. And keep an eye on anything unusual in the neighborhood. Anything at all, report it to the police."

She offered a small, reassuring smile. "Thanks for your time, Jack. I'll get back to you as soon as I have something."

As Blue turned to leave, her face remained composed, a practiced mask hiding the undercurrent of worry that Jack's situation had stirred within her. Her steps away from his house were measured, leaving no trace of the concern that weighed on her mind.

Chapter Nine

Blue pulled up to Ethan's house just as the sun was beginning to set. He was waiting on the porch, a look of anticipation on his face. As he climbed into the passenger seat of her car, he gave her a warm smile.

"Hey, Blue," he greeted, buckling his seatbelt as she pulled away from the curb. "How did it go with Jack?"

Blue sighed, her mind still spinning from the day's events. "It was... interesting," she began, deciding to start with the surveillance camera. She recounted her discovery of the camera in the bushes and how they had watched the footage but couldn't identify anyone.

Ethan's brow furrowed in concern as he listened. "That's unsettling. Do you think it's related to Tom's death?"

"I'm not sure," Blue admitted. "But it's definitely suspicious. Jack seemed genuinely scared."

Their conversation continued as they drove to The Rusty Nail, a popular bar in town known for its laidback atmosphere and good food. Once they arrived and found a corner table, they ordered food and drinks, and Blue filled Ethan in on Detective Jameson's visit to the candy shop.

"I've never heard of a Detective Jameson," Ethan said, echoing what Brock had told her earlier. "And his approach was definitely unorthodox. Detectives usually don't leave cryptic notes for people to find."

Blue nodded, pulling out the note from her pocket and placing it on the table. "This is what he left. It's vague and doesn't give much away."

Ethan studied the note, his eyes scanning the hastily scrawled words. "It's definitely strange. But it could also be a trap. We should be careful."

Blue agreed, feeling a chill run down her spine. "I don't plan on walking into a potential trap blindly. That's why I asked you to come with me."

Ethan gave her a reassuring smile. "I'm glad you did. We'll figure this out together."

As they waited for their food, they speculated about who could be behind the surveillance on Jack's house. They considered several possibilities, including Tom's killer, someone with a grudge against Jack, or even a private investigator hired by someone in town.

"Regardless of who it is, we need to find out why they're watching Jack," Blue said, her determination shining through. "He's clearly scared, and I don't blame him."

After they finished their meal, Blue and Ethan sat in silence, their eyes scanning the crowd for any sign of the mysterious Detective Jameson. But as the minutes turned into an hour, it became clear that they had been stood up. No one was coming to meet Blue.

Blue sighed, her fingers tracing the rim of her empty glass. "I had a feeling this might happen," she confessed, her voice barely above a whisper. "Something about Jameson didn't sit right with me."

Ethan leaned back in his chair, his gaze thoughtful. "I agree. His approach was unorthodox, and leaving a cryptic note instead of directly contacting you is suspicious. But we shouldn't jump to conclusions just yet."

Blue nodded, appreciating Ethan's levelheadedness. "You're right. We need more information before we can make any judgments."

Ethan's eyes lit up, a spark of determination in his gaze. "I can help with that. I have some resources we can use to dig deeper into Jameson's background."

With that, they left The Rusty Nail and drove to Ethan's office, a small but well-equipped space filled with computers and various investigative tools. Ethan quickly got to work, his fingers flying over the keyboard as he searched for any information on a Detective Jameson.

After a few minutes, he turned to Blue, his expression serious. "I can confirm that Jameson isn't a detective. At least, not any detective that I can find records of."

Blue felt a chill run down her spine. "So, he's an imposter?"

Ethan shrugged, his eyes still on the screen. "It seems so. But beyond that, I don't know much more about him yet. His trail is well covered."

Blue nodded, her mind racing with possibilities. "We need to be careful, Ethan. If he's not a detective, then who knows what he's capable of."

Ethan agreed, his gaze meeting hers. "We'll find out who he is, Blue. And we'll figure out what he wants."

Feeling the weight of their discovery, Blue decided they needed a break from the heavy atmosphere. "Let's lighten the mood a bit," she suggested, her eyes sparkling with a sudden idea. "I've been working on a new line of candies at Sucre Bleu. Would you like to be a tester?"

Ethan looked surprised but quickly agreed, intrigued by the offer. "I'd love to. I've always had a sweet tooth."

What Blue didn't tell him was that these weren't just any candies. They were infused with subtle magic, a secret she wasn't ready to reveal just yet.

They left Ethan's office and made their way back to Sucre Bleu. Blue led him to the back of the shop, where she kept her latest creations. She handed him a small, beautifully wrapped candy. "Try this," she said. "It's a rosemary candy."

Ethan unwrapped the candy and popped it into his mouth. His eyes widened in surprise. "This is amazing, Blue," he said, savoring the unique flavor. "The rosemary is subtle but distinct. It's unlike anything I've ever tasted."

Blue couldn't help but smile at his reaction. "I'm glad you like it. I've been thinking about creating a line of 'herbal' candies. Different flavors, different ingredients, each with their own unique effects and benefits."

Ethan was intrigued. "That sounds like a fantastic idea. You could experiment with lavender, mint, basil... the possibilities are endless."

As they delved deeper into the brainstorming session, Blue found herself increasingly engrossed in the potential of her magical candies. The idea, initially suggested by Pepper, of creating magical candies for the shop was starting to take root in her mind. The possibilities seemed endless, and the thought of it filled her with a sense of exhilaration.

"What about chamomile?" Ethan suggested, his eyes sparkling with enthusiasm. "It's known for its calming properties. Could be a hit for those seeking a bit of tranquility."

Blue nodded, her mind already racing with ideas. "That's brilliant, Ethan. And maybe we could pair it with honey. A chamomile-honey candy for relaxation. I love it!"

As they continued to toss ideas back and forth, Blue found herself watching Ethan more closely. His face was animated, his eyes bright with curiosity and excitement. She noticed the way his lips curved into a smile when he came up with a new idea, the way his eyes crinkled at the corners when he laughed. She felt a flutter in her stomach, a warmth spreading through her. Was this just friendly camaraderie, or was there a hint of something more?

Ethan seemed to sense her gaze, turning to meet her eyes. There was a pause, a moment of silence that felt charged with unspoken words. Blue quickly looked away, a blush creeping up her cheeks. Could there be a potential romance brewing between them?

The evening had settled in, and Sucre Bleu was officially closed for business. However, the warm, inviting lights of the candy shop remained on, illuminating the quiet street outside. Inside, Blue and Ethan were engrossed in their candy-making experiment, their laughter and conversation filling the otherwise silent shop.

Their focus was interrupted when the door creaked open, the sound echoing through the shop. Kimber stepped in. Her usual vibrant energy was replaced with a tired and frustrated demeanor. Her eyes, usually sparkling with life, were now red-rimmed and weary. Her shoulders, typically held high with confidence, were slumped in defeat.

Blue glanced at the clock hanging on the wall, noting the late hour. However, seeing Kimber's state, she couldn't bring herself to tell her they were closed. Instead, she gestured for Kimber to join them at the counter, where they were surrounded by an array of candy ingredients, molds, and experimental concoctions.

Kimber moved to the counter, her steps slow and heavy. She stood there, her fingers absently tracing the edge of a candy mold as she began to share her frustrations about Tom. Her voice wavered with a mix of anger and sorrow, the words tumbling out in a rush. Blue listened attentively, her heart aching for Kimber's situation.

As Kimber began to delve deeper into her story, a disturbing detail emerged. Her voice, usually so full of life, was now laced with a tremor of fear and frustration. "Detective Jameson...he's been...he's been harassing me," she confessed, her fingers tightening around the edge of the counter.

Blue and Ethan exchanged a glance, their attention fully on Kimber. "Harassing you? How?" Blue asked, her voice filled with concern.

Kimber's eyes darted to the floor, her grip on the counter tightening. "He's been...he's been trying to make me confess to...to Tom's murder," she stammered, the words tumbling out in a rush. Her eyes flickered up to meet Blue's, a desperate plea for understanding in them. "But I didn't...I didn't do it, Blue. I swear."

Blue exchanged a glance with Ethan, her mind racing. She turned back to Kimber, her voice gentle but steady. "Kimber," she said, "Jameson isn't a real detective."

Kimber looked up, surprise flickering across her face. "What?"

Blue nodded, repeating her words for emphasis. "He's not a detective. Ethan did some investigating. We don't know much about him yet, but we know that much."

A wave of relief washed over Kimber's face, and she let out a shaky laugh. "So, I can just ignore him?"

Blue nodded again. "Or better yet, call Brock the next time he bothers you. He's a real detective, and he can handle Jameson."

Kimber expressed her gratitude, her words a soft sigh of relief. The tension that had been coiled tightly in her shoulders seemed to dissipate, replaced by a weary resignation. She bid them a quiet goodbye and exited the shop, the door closing gently behind her.

Blue and Ethan were left standing in the comforting, sugary-scented warmth of Sucre Bleu. The soft glow from the candy displays cast a serene light around them, a stark contrast to the turmoil that had just unfolded.

As the echo of the closing door faded, Blue found herself enveloped in a sense of unease. The enigma that was Jameson was proving to be more complex than they had initially thought. His actions were not just suspicious, they were dangerous. She glanced at Ethan, his face a mirror of her own concern. She knew then they had to unravel this mystery, not just for their sake, but for Kimber's as well.

Feeling a surge of determination, Blue decided that it was time to take a more direct approach in dealing with Jameson. Ethan, with his myriad of connections and resources, managed to secure a phone number for the elusive man. They remained within the comforting, familiar surroundings of Ethan's office as Blue dialed the number, her heart pounding a rhythm of anticipation and apprehension in her chest.

"Jameson," she began, her voice steady despite the nerves fluttering in her stomach, "I think it's time we had a conversation about Tom's murder."

She suggested a face-to-face meeting, emphasizing her expectation that he would honor the arrangement this time. Jameson, sounding slightly surprised by her forthrightness, agreed to the meeting. However, he stipulated one condition: she had to come alone, without Ethan, whom he dismissively referred to as "the giant brick wall of a man."

Blue assured him that she would attend the meeting solo, and they settled on a local cafe as the venue. Her intention was to scrutinize him closely during their interaction, hoping to pick up on any subtle cues or reactions that might provide insight into his role in the unfolding mystery.

Ethan, concerned about her safety, advised her to proceed with caution. He proposed that he accompany her to the cafe, not to directly participate in the meeting, but to keep a watchful eye from a discreet distance. Blue agreed to this arrangement, suspecting that Ethan's presence during their previous encounter might have been what deterred Jameson.

"All right," she conceded, "you can come along. But you'll have to find a spot somewhere else in the cafe. We don't want to risk scaring him off again."

Chapter Ten

The local café was a symphony of clinking dishes, murmured conversations, and the rich aroma of freshly brewed coffee. Blue had chosen a booth that offered a clear view of the entrance, her heart pounding with a mix of anticipation and apprehension. Ethan had taken a seat in the booth directly behind hers, his back to the room. His auburn hair, usually a beacon, was tucked under a nondescript hat, making him blend in with the other patrons.

The café door swung open, causing a gust of wind to sweep through the room. Jameson stepped inside, his eyes scanning the café before they landed on Blue. He walked over, seemingly oblivious to Ethan's presence. The hostess, with a polite smile, guided him to Blue's booth.

"Detective Jameson," Blue responded, her voice steady despite the nerves fluttering in her stomach. She steered the conversation towards the topic at hand. "I wanted to talk to you about Tom's murder."

Jameson's face remained impassive, his eyes guarded. "I'm not sure what you think I can tell you," he said, his voice measured.

Blue persisted, her gaze never leaving his face. "You knew Tom, didn't you?"

A flicker of something crossed Jameson's face. "We had... business together," he admitted, a bitter twist to his lips.

"Business?" Blue probed. "What kind of business?"

Jameson hesitated, his gaze shifting away from Blue's intense stare. "It's... complicated," he said, his voice strained.

Blue leaned in, her voice soft but insistent. "Jameson, if you know something that could help solve Tom's murder, you need to tell me."

Jameson sighed, running a hand through his hair. He looked at Blue, his eyes filled with a mix of regret and resignation. "It was an... illicit venture," he confessed, his voice barely above a whisper. "We were involved in some... questionable activities."

"And?" Blue prompted, her heart pounding in her chest.

Jameson looked down, his voice barely audible over the café's background noise. "It ended badly. Ruined me financially."

The revelation hit Blue like a punch to the gut. Could this financial ruin have been a motive for murder? And why was he admitting this? If he was admitting this so easily, was there more that was even worse?

As the conversation continued, Blue began to weave a delicate web of half-truths and insinuations. She dropped hints about her knowledge of Jameson's past business venture with Tom, carefully watching his reactions.

"You know, I've heard some things about Tom's business partner," she began, her voice casual. "Some say he was the brains behind the operation."

Jameson's eyes flickered, a hint of unease creeping into his expression. "Is that so?" he asked, his voice tight.

Blue nodded, maintaining her nonchalant demeanor. "Yes, apparently this partner was quite the strategist. Managed to keep his hands clean while Tom did the dirty work."

Jameson shifted uncomfortably in his seat, his gaze darting around the café. "I wouldn't know anything about that," he said, his voice defensive.

Blue pressed on, her voice steady. "Well, it's just what I've heard. Apparently, this partner would be the one who would do real prison time, because he was the one who masterminded everything illegal. Sounds like a tough break."

Jameson's face paled, his eyes wide. "I... I don't know what you're talking about," he stammered, his voice barely above a whisper.

Blue leaned back in her seat, her gaze never leaving Jameson's face. "Of course, it's all just rumors," she said, her voice soft. "But it does make one wonder, doesn't it?"

Jameson was silent for a moment, his gaze fixed on the table. He seemed to be wrestling with something, his mind clearly churning. Finally, he looked up at Blue, his eyes filled with a mix of fear and defiance. "I don't know what you're trying to imply, but I had nothing to do with Tom's death."

Blue simply nodded, her expression unreadable. "I'm sure you didn't, Jameson. But it's always good to clear the air, isn't it?"

Jameson's face was a mask of desperation as he continued to plead his case. "I didn't know, Blue. I swear, I didn't know what Tom was getting us into," he insisted, his voice shaking slightly. "When I found out... when I realized what we were doing was illegal... I got out as fast as I could."

Blue watched him, her expression softening. She reached across the table, placing her hand over his in a gesture of comfort. "I believe you, Jameson," she said, her voice filled with empathy. "It sounds like you were caught in a difficult situation."

Jameson looked at her, his eyes filled with relief. "You have no idea, Blue," he said, his voice choked with emotion. "I've been living with this guilt, this fear... it's been unbearable."

Blue gave his hand a reassuring squeeze. "I can only imagine how hard it's been for you," she said, her voice gentle. "But you're not alone, Jameson. You can trust me."

Jameson nodded, his eyes welling up with tears. "Thank you, Blue," he said, his voice barely above a whisper. "I... I don't know why I've been doing the things I've been doing. I just have to find a way to make things right."

Blue smiled at him, her heart pounding in her chest. She was playing a dangerous game, but she was willing to take the risk if it meant getting closer to the truth. She would continue to play the sympathetic friend, hoping that Jameson would let his guard down and reveal more about his involvement with Tom's illicit activities.

The sudden vibration of Blue's phone on the table broke the tense atmosphere that had settled between her and Jameson. She glanced at the screen, seeing Pepper's name flash across it. She felt a twinge of relief, an excuse to end the increasingly uncomfortable conversation.

"I'm sorry, Jameson," she said, her voice laced with a feigned regret. "I need to take this. It's my assistant. She's a bit of a handful sometimes."

Jameson's eyebrows lifted slightly, but he nodded, leaning back in his seat. "Of course, go ahead."

Blue picked up the phone, pressing it to her ear. "Pepper, what's going on?" she asked, her eyes never leaving Jameson, watching his every reaction.

"Blue, you won't believe it!" Pepper's voice was a whirlwind of excitement. "I've managed to create a magical candy prototype. You have to come back to the shop and try it!"

Blue blinked, taken aback by the unexpected news. She hadn't anticipated this development because she didn't even know Pepper was at the candy shop. She must have gotten bored at home alone. "That's... that's fantastic, Pepper. I'll be there as soon as I can."

She turned back to Jameson, her expression apologetic. "I'm sorry, Jameson, but I need to go. We've had a bit of a breakthrough at the shop, and I need to handle it."

"Of course, Blue. We'll talk later."

Blue rose from her seat. She offered Jameson a courteous smile, her thoughts already racing ahead to the next phase of their investigation. "I appreciate your time, Jameson. I'm sure we'll have more to discuss soon."

He responded with a nod, his eyes tracking her as she navigated her way through the café. She could feel the weight of his gaze on her, but she maintained a steady stride, her face a mask of calm. Once outside, she welcomed the cool air that brushed against her skin, a refreshing contrast to the tense atmosphere she had just left behind.

She stole a quick glance back through the café window, spotting Ethan's broad back still hunched over his table, his auburn hair hidden beneath a hat. She swiftly pulled out her phone, her fingers dancing over the screen as she composed a message to Ethan. 'Join me at the shop when you can,' she typed, before tucking her phone back into her pocket. She didn't want to arouse Jameson's suspicion by leaving with Ethan, but she hope Ethan would come to the shop when he could leave.

***

The quaint chime of the doorbell echoed through the candy shop as Blue gingerly pushed open the entrance to Sucre Bleu. The familiar, comforting scent of caramelizing sugar and warming spices enveloped her, instantly washing away the tension from her meeting with Jameson. The shop was a sanctuary, a place of warmth and sweetness that never failed to bring her solace.

Pepper was hunched over the counter at the back of the shop, her usually wild curls tamed into a neat bun. Her face was lit up with a kind of excitement that Blue hadn't seen in a while. As Blue approached, Pepper looked up, her eyes sparkling like two sapphires.

"Blue, you're back!" Pepper's voice rang out, echoing around the shop. She held out a small piece of candy, its surface shimmering under the soft lighting of the shop. "You have to try this."

Blue reached out and took the candy from Pepper. It was a small, delicate thing, beautifully crafted and filled with a gentle pulsating magic. She could feel the energy emanating from it, a soft hum that tingled against her skin. Without a second thought, she popped it into her mouth.

The candy melted on her tongue, releasing a burst of sweetness that made her taste buds dance. Almost instantly, she felt a surge of positive energy coursing through her veins. Her senses heightened, the world around her seemed to come alive. The colors of the shop became more vibrant, the sounds more distinct, and the scent of the shop more intoxicating.

Pepper was watching her with bated breath, her eyes wide with anticipation. "Well?" she asked, her voice barely a whisper, her hands clasped together in front of her.

Blue turned to her, a slow smile spreading across her face. "Pepper," she said, her voice filled with awe and wonder, "it's incredible."

Pepper let out a squeal of delight, her whole body bouncing with excitement. "I knew it! I knew it would work!"

Blue couldn't help but laugh, her heart swelling with pride for her sister. She looked around the shop, her gaze sweeping over the rows of candies displayed in the glass cases. She could see it now - a new line of magical candies, each one designed to enhance the lives of their customers in some way. It was a bold idea, but one that held so much potential.

"Pepper," she said, turning back to her sister, her eyes shining with determination. "I think we're onto something big here. Let's do this. Let's make magical candies for Sucre Bleu."

Pepper's grin was infectious, her excitement palpable. "Absolutely, Blue. Let's make magic."

***

The shop was quiet, save for the soft murmur of conversation between Blue and Pepper. They were huddled together at one of the tables, a piece of parchment spread out before them, their heads bent in deep discussion.

Blue's eyes were alight with a fervor that only came when she was excited about a new idea. "Just think about it, Pepper," she said, her voice filled with enthusiasm. "Candies that do more than just satisfy a craving. Candies that can actually enhance your mood, your senses, your overall well-being."

Pepper's eyes sparkled with excitement as she caught on to her sister's vision. "We could create candies for relaxation, for focus, for happiness," she chimed in, her mind already whirring with potential recipes. "The possibilities are truly endless!"

Their brainstorming session was interrupted by the soft jingle of the shop's doorbell. They both looked up to see Ethan walking in, his face serious and his eyes focused. He held a manila folder in his hands, and Blue instantly knew he had found something significant.

"Ethan," Blue greeted, her voice filled with a mix of anticipation and apprehension. "What did you find?"

Ethan took a deep breath, his gaze meeting Blue's. "I stopped by my office before coming here," he began, his voice steady. "I did some more digging into Jameson's past."

Blue leaned forward, her heart pounding in her chest. "And?" she prompted.

Ethan opened the folder, revealing a series of documents. "I found evidence linking Jameson to a number of illegal activities," he revealed, his voice grave. "And there are definite connections to Tom."

Blue's eyes widened in surprise. "That's what he hinted at during our meeting," she admitted, her mind racing. "He was vague and blamed everything on Tom, but I had a feeling there was more to it."

Ethan nodded, his expression serious. "I heard the conversation. That's why I felt the need to dig deeper. And it looks like we were right to be suspicious."

Blue took a moment to process the information, her mind whirling with the implications. "So, what do we do now?" she asked.

Ethan looked at her, his gaze steady and resolute. "I think we need to have another talk with our 'detective' friend," he said, his voice firm. "And this time, we'll be prepared."

Chapter Eleven

After ensuring that Pepper was safely home and tucked in for the night, Blue and Ethan settled at the kitchen table, their laptops open before them. The room was filled with the soft hum of their computers and the occasional clink of their mugs as they sipped on hot cocoa, a comforting presence amidst the tension of their investigation.

Ethan, with his background as a private investigator, had access to a wealth of resources and databases that Blue could only dream of. He navigated through them with ease, his fingers flying over the keyboard as he delved into the depths of Derek Jameson's past.

Blue watched him work, her own screen filled with search results and articles about Jameson. She was also looking into his financial transactions, trying to find any irregularities or suspicious activities that could link him to Tom's murder. Every so often, she would glance over at Ethan, taking in his focused expression and the way his brow furrowed in concentration.

As the hours ticked by, they began to piece together a picture of Jameson's shady business dealings. There were numerous transactions that didn't add up, connections to people with criminal records, and a trail of financial ruin that seemed to follow him wherever he went.

Ethan was the one who found the first concrete piece of evidence. "Look at this," he said, his voice breaking the silence. He turned his laptop so Blue could see the screen.

It was a bank statement, showing a large sum of money transferred from Jameson's account to an offshore one, just days before Tom's murder.

Blue's mind raced as she took in the information. This was it. This was the evidence they needed. She looked at Ethan, her eyes wide with realization. "We need to take this to the police," she said, her voice filled with determination. "We need to bring Jameson to justice."

Ethan's expression shifted, his brows furrowing in concern. "Blue, we can't just take this to the police," he said, his voice filled with a mix of caution and regret.

Blue looked at him, taken aback. "What do you mean, we can't? Ethan, this is evidence. This could link Jameson to Tom's murder."

Ethan ran a hand through his hair, a gesture of frustration. "Firstly," he began, "I'm not entirely sure it's legal for me to let you use these financial tracing resources. I have access to them as a private investigator but sharing them with you... it's a gray area, at best."

Blue opened her mouth to protest, but Ethan held up a hand to stop her. "And secondly," he continued, "this bank transfer is interesting, yes, but it's not concrete evidence. It's a lead, a strong one, but it's not enough to prove Jameson's guilt. We need more."

Blue fell silent, her excitement deflating. She looked at the bank statement on the screen, her mind racing. Ethan was right. They needed more evidence, something undeniable that could link Jameson to Tom's murder. But where would they find it?

"We'll keep digging," Ethan said, his voice soft but resolved. "We'll find the evidence we need, Blue. We just need to be patient and thorough."

***

The peppermint tea warmed Blue from the inside out as she sipped it slowly. She savored the soothing minty flavor, the heat from the ceramic mug pleasantly seeping into her palms. It had been a long day of chasing lead after lead, only to hit dead end after dead end in her investigation into Tom's murder. The cozy warmth and sweet scent of the candy shop was a welcome respite from the bitter chill that perpetually lingered in the late autumn air.

She glanced up as the bronze shop bell jingled brightly, announcing the arrival of a customer. A young woman with cascading waves of golden blonde hair entered the shop. She had a nervous energy about her, anxiously wringing her hands as her shifty gaze darted around the interior of the shop. Despite the gloomy weather outside, she wore large black sunglasses that obscured most of her face.

As the woman hovered near the entrance, seemingly working up the nerve to step further inside, Blue studied her curiously. There was something familiar about her, though Blue couldn't quite place where she had seen this mysterious visitor before.

"Can I help you find something?" Blue finally asked, hoping to break the awkward tension.

The woman visibly started at the sound of Blue's voice, as if lost in her own worrisome thoughts. "Oh, uh, no. No, I'm not here to, uh... I don't need any candy."

Blue's brows knit together in confusion. It wasn't often someone wandered into a candy shop without intending to make a purchase. "Are you sure? We've got a great selection of chocolates, taffies, gummies..."

"No, really, I just..." The woman trailed off again, biting her lip apprehensively. After a heavy silence, she spoke again, her voice barely above a whisper. "I have some information. About the murder."

Blue's eyes widened in surprise, and she nearly spilled her steaming tea in her haste to set the mug down on the counter. She leaned forward intently, heart hammering with anticipation. "You know something about Tom Wiseman's murder?"

The blonde woman cast another furtive glance around the shop, as if double checking they were alone. Apparently satisfied, she replied softly, "It's about that detective you've been dealing with. Jameson."

Blue inhaled sharply. This mysterious visitor clearly knew more about the situation than she was letting on. "What about him? Did you see something?" Blue pressed.

The woman gave a quick nod, her fingers worrying the strap of her purse. "Yeah. Yeah, I saw him two nights ago.

He was at that storage facility on the edge of town, you know, the one right off Route 5."

"You saw Jameson at the storage facility? What was he doing?" Blue could barely contain her eagerness, hungry for any new information related to Jameson and his suspicious activities.

"He was going into one of the units. Looked real paranoid, kept checking over his shoulder before he unlocked the door." The woman leaned in, dropping her voice lower. "He was definitely up to something shady. Stayed in there a long time."

Blue's pulse quickened, her investigative instincts kicking into overdrive. This could be the lead they needed to finally unravel this mystery. "Did you see what was inside the unit? Or what he was doing in there?"

The blonde woman shook her head, twisting a lock of hair around her finger distractedly. "Nah, couldn't see anything once he went in and pulled the door down. But he was in there at least an hour or so. Seemed like he was looking for something specific."

She shifted her weight from foot to foot, clearly anxious to provide her tip and slip away unnoticed. But Blue wasn't ready to let her disappear just yet. There were still so many questions swirling through her mind.

"I don't suppose you happened to notice the unit number?" Blue asked hopefully. "Or anything else that could help pinpoint the exact one?"

The woman chewed her lip thoughtfully for a moment before shaking her head. "Unit 1138."

Blue offered an appreciative smile. "Thank you. I really do appreciate you coming here to tell me this. Anything we can find out about Jameson's activities could be crucial."

The blonde woman nodded, the hint of a smile playing at her lips. "Yeah, no problem. I just want to see that creep get what's coming to him." She glanced anxiously at the clock on the wall. "Anyway, I should get going."

"Wait!" Blue exclaimed as the woman turned abruptly toward the exit. "Before you go, can you tell me your name? In case I need to follow up on anything?"

The woman froze with her hand on the door, hesitating a moment. "Uh, it's better if I don't say," she finally muttered. Before Blue could protest, she pushed the door open and hurried out of the shop, the bell jangling sharply in her wake.

Blue stood motionless behind the counter, stunned by the bizarre encounter. Her mind raced as she processed the intriguing new lead. A storage unit connected to Jameson? It was too enticing to ignore. She had to tell Ethan immediately.

Fishing her phone out of her back pocket, she quickly typed out a message. "We need to check out a storage facility on Route 5. I just got an anonymous tip that Jameson was seen going into a unit there a couple nights ago. This could be big!"

She drummed her fingers impatiently on the countertop as she awaited Ethan's response. After a few tense moments, her phone dinged with an incoming text.

"On my way. Be there in ten." Even through text, she could detect the undercurrent of excitement in Ethan's terse response. He clearly sensed this could be the breakthrough they'd been waiting for.

Blue tidied up the shop in preparation to close early, anticipation and apprehension swirling within her. This felt like more than just another lead. Her witchy intuition, the internal voice she'd learned long ago not to ignore, told her that storage unit held answers.

Precisely ten minutes later, the low rumble of a motorcycle could be heard approaching outside. Moments later, Ethan strode through the door, the scent of leather and engine grease trailing him. He ran a hand through his perpetually tousled auburn hair, his sapphire eyes alight with curiosity.

"You said something about a storage unit? And Jameson being connected to it?" He rubbed his hands together briskly, unable to contain his eagerness. "What are we waiting for, let's go check it out!"

Blue quickly relayed the minimal details from her puzzling interaction with the mystery woman as she grabbed her purse and keys. Ethan's expression turned stormy at the mention of Jameson, his jaw clenching and shoulders tensing.

"If that snake is stashing things in a secret storage unit, it can't mean anything good," he muttered darkly. "We need to find out what he's hiding."

Blue flipped the "Closed" sign on the shop door and locked it securely before climbing into the driver's seat of her car. Ethan folded himself into the passenger side, the aged leather creaking beneath his muscular frame. The engine rumbled to life, and they pulled away from the curb to begin the short drive to the storage facility.

As Blue maneuvered the car along the rural backroads leading out of town, she recounted her strange interaction again for Ethan's benefit. He listened intently, shaking his head in frustration.

"I don't like that she refused to identify herself," he said. "Makes it seem like she has something to hide."

"I agree it's odd," Blue conceded. "But she seemed genuinely scared. Like she knew revealing herself would put her in danger."

Ethan made a thoughtful noise in his throat. "Maybe. Or it could be someone connected to Jameson trying to send us on a wild-goose chase."

Blue gripped the steering wheel tighter, not having considered that possibility. Was this phantom tipster truly trying to help, or deliberately feeding them false information? There was only one way to find out.

Dusk was just beginning to settle over the landscape as they turned onto Route 5. The mammoth self-storage facility could be spotted a ways down the road, the rows of identical metal units glittering under the streetlights like tin soldiers standing at attention.

Blue reduced her speed as they pulled into the sprawling complex, carefully scanning the numbers affixed beside each roll-up door. They crawled through the maze of corridors until Blue finally tapped the brakes, nodding toward one of the units.

"There," she said. Unit 1138 loomed before them, its sturdy padlock and door betraying no clues about its contents. Blue killed the engine, staring at the innocuous unit with a mix of anticipation and hesitation churning within her.

Ethan eyed the solid padlock securing the unit, a wry smile tugging at his lips. "Well, it's locked up nice and tight. But I think I can handle that." He reached into the interior pocket of his worn leather jacket, withdrawing a small leather case. It opened to reveal an array of delicate tools.

Blue watched in fascination as Ethan selected two slender pieces and went to work manipulating the lock's inner mechanisms. His brow furrowed in concentration, tongue poking from the corner of his mouth as he maneuvered the precision instruments. After several moments of tense silence, there was a faint but audible click, and the padlock sprang open.

"We're in business," Ethan murmured with satisfaction as he removed the padlock and pocketed his tools. Gripping the handle built into the bottom of the rolling door, he slowly slid it upward to reveal the darkened space within.

The musty scent of stale air and dust wafted out. Blue fumbled to retrieve the mini flashlight attached to her keyring, flicking it on to produce a narrow beam. She swept the pale circle of light back and forth over the unit's cluttered interior.

The ten-by-fifteen space was crammed haphazardly with an odd assortment of boxes, furniture, and other unidentifiable items shrouded in tarps and shadows. Cautiously, Blue took a step inside, Ethan close on her heels. He pulled a small LED flashlight from his own keychain, adding more illumination as they peered into the gloomy corners.

"What a mess," Blue muttered, noting the lack of organization. "Finding anything in this disaster will be like searching for a needle in a haystack."

They inched deeper into the cramped unit, meticulously inspecting their surroundings. As Blue's light glinted off a battered old desk tucked against the far wall, her breath caught in her throat. Barely visible from her vantage point was the unmistakable glint of a detective's badge peeking out from a coat slung over the chair.

"Jackpot," Ethan exclaimed under his breath as he focused his light on the same spot. They exchanged a charged look, the air suddenly crackling with electricity. This was it. They had found his hideout.

Blue could scarcely breathe, her nerves and excitement reaching a fever pitch. A dozen questions careened through her mind as adrenaline flooded her veins. What else might Jameson have stashed in this secret lair? What clues could it hold to finally unraveling this mystery?

With renewed vigor, they pressed deeper into the shadowy recesses of the storage unit. Each item they encountered was subjected to thorough scrutiny as they hunted for further evidence. Under the desk, they found a locked briefcase that Ethan swiftly picked open, revealing stacks of files brimming with incriminating documents.

Behind a floor lamp with a missing shade, Blue unearthed a paper grocery bag containing several disposable cell phones. A wooden crate wedged in the back corner held an assortment of license plates from various states. They meticulously sifted through the accumulating pile of discoveries, snapping photos of each item.

Blue's skin prickled with exhilaration and uncertainty. What had begun as a hunch was snowballing into a trove of undeniable proof of Jameson's deceitful schemes.

"This stuff has to link him to Tom's murder somehow," Ethan declared as they continue to root through the treasure trove. "Why else would he have a secret storage unit filled with burner phones and fake IDs?"

Blue delved back into the clutter with renewed zeal. They still had some digging to do, but she could feel they were on the cusp of a major breakthrough. The truth was here somewhere, buried amidst the contents of this unassuming storage unit. She would not rest until it was unearthed.

Chapter Twelve

Adrenaline coursed through Blue's veins as she snapped photo after photo of the incriminating evidence they had uncovered. Her phone's camera rolled continuously, capturing every detail of Jameson's secret stash. Beside her, Ethan was engrossed in photographing the contents of the briefcase they had discovered.

Time seemed to fade into the background as they became absorbed in their task, driven by the prospect that the next item moved or box opened could reveal the vital piece of evidence needed to link Jameson to Tom's murder.

Blue was crouched on the concrete floor, peeling back layers of clutter to reveal a hidden cache of suspicious financial records. Her knees ached and her neck cramped from hovering over her phone's screen, but she pushed any discomfort aside, too invested in her search to stop.

As she reached for another bundle of papers tied with fraying twine, Ethan suddenly grasped her shoulder. "Someone's coming!" he hissed under his breath.

Blue froze, ears straining. Sure enough, she could just make out the scuff of approaching footsteps over the hammering of her own heartbeat.

In unspoken agreement, they hastily shoved the scattered evidence back under the desk and switched off their flashlight beams. Moving as one, they darted toward the darkest corner of the cramped unit, huddling together behind a moldy sofa.

Peering through a gap in the stained cushions, Blue watched with bated breath as the door rattled upward, letting in a slice of hazy evening light. Two shadowy figures shuffled inside, their faces obscured by the backlighting.

Blue's muscles tensed, braced for confrontation. But the newcomers seemed oblivious to her and Ethan's presence. They fanned out, beginning to rummage through the cluttered space.

She strained to make out their muffled conversation, pressing closer to the gap in the sofa. One voice she recognized immediately as Jameson's low gravelly tone. The other man was unfamiliar, his words too faint to decipher.

Her mind raced. What were they doing here? Had Jameson realized his unit had been disturbed? A cold trickle of fear snaked down Blue's spine. If they were caught, there was no telling how Jameson might react.

Beside her, Ethan was stock-still, barely breathing. His solid frame radiated warmth and tension as he tracked the men's movements. Blue kept her eyes glued to the open door, praying for them to leave so she and Ethan could slip away undetected.

After what felt like an eternity of anxious waiting, she detected a slight shift in Jameson's demeanor. His posture changed, shoulders tightening as his voice took on a sharp edge that pierced the gloom.

"It's got to be here somewhere," Jameson rasped, raking a hand through his hair in agitation. He began yanking boxes from shelves, rifling through their contents before hurling them aside. "We can't leave until we find it."

His companion, face still obscured, rested a hand on Jameson's arm placatingly. "Hey, take it easy," he soothed. "We'll keep looking, but trashing this place isn't going to help."

Jameson shrugged him off but seemed to regain a sliver of composure. They resumed their search with renewed intensity, overturning furniture and going through boxes in their quest for the unspecified object.

Crammed in that airless, lightless space behind the sofa, Blue's nerves were frayed to the breaking point. Her lungs strained for steady breaths, fearful the slightest sound would give them away. Just when she thought she couldn't take the suspense any longer, Jameson uttered a triumphant exclamation.

"Aha, got it!" He held up a nondescript manila envelope, clutching it with feverish intensity. Blue strained to see what it contained.

A tense silence descended on the storage unit after Jameson's discovery of the mystery envelope. Blue scarcely dared to breathe, pinned in that cramped, airless space behind the moth-eaten sofa. Beside her, Ethan was coiled tight as a spring, his stormy eyes tracking Jameson's every movement.

Jameson stood slightly hunched, turning the unmarked envelope over in his hands with an almost reverent delicacy. His companion looked on over his shoulder, brow furrowed.

"You really think that's everything?" the unnamed man asked. His voice was a low rumble, each word slow and deliberate.

Jameson didn't reply right away, still wholly fixated on the envelope clutched to his chest. After an interminable pause, he finally spoke, his own gravelly voice barely above a whisper.

"It has to be. This is everything he had on me." Jameson's tongue darted out, wetting his cracked lips. "Which means there's only one thing left to do now."

The other man tilted his head, a wary look creeping over his face. "And what's that?"

Jameson turned, his profile visible to Blue even in the dimness. The set of his jaw and feverish glint in his eyes sent a chill skittering down her spine.

"Tie up loose ends," he uttered coldly. "Permanently."

Blue's breath caught, dread congealing in her veins. Beside her, Ethan had gone utterly motionless, tuned like a laser to Jameson's every syllable.

Oblivious to their unseen audience, Jameson pressed on, his voice taking on a sharper edge. "That means we've got some messes that need cleaning up. Starting with that shifty secretary, what's-her-name."

"You mean Carrie?" the second man interjected. "She's harmless, barely knows anything."

Jameson whirled, his eyes blazing. "Exactly, she doesn't know anything yet. But it's only a matter of time before she starts poking around, asking questions." He turned his gaze upward, as if lost in thought. "Better to take care of it now, before she becomes a problem."

The other man shifted his weight, clearly uneasy. "Take care of it? You don't mean..."

"I do," Jameson cut him off curtly. "It's the only way. Believe me, it's better this way. We can't leave any threads dangling." He began to pace, movements jagged and erratic. "And she's not the only one. That nosy reporter too, what's his name..."

"You're talking about Elijah?" The man's voice rose in pitch, disbelief etched on his face. "Now hang on, we never agreed-"

"Enough!" Jameson roared, slamming his fist against the desk. The echo reverberated through the confined space. Behind the sofa, Blue jolted at the sudden violence, her heart stuttering frantically.

Jameson stood trembling, sucking in gulping breaths as he sought to regain composure. When he continued, his voice was ice cold and razor sharp.

"I've worked too hard and sacrificed too much to let it all unravel now. If you're not prepared to do what's necessary, then you're a liability." His lip curled derisively. "I can easily find someone who is."

131

A ringing silence followed his words. The nameless man seemed to shrink into himself under Jameson's ruthless stare. After an agonizing pause, he gave the barest of nods.

Jameson clapped him on the back. "Good man," he praised, previous chilliness vanishing as quickly as it had come. "This is for the best. You'll see."

Turning on his heel, Jameson strode for the door, envelope tucked close against his side. His footfalls echoed like shotgun blasts in Blue's ears until the door rattled shut, cloaking the unit in musty blackness once more.

For a split second, everything was static and still. Then Ethan exploded into motion beside Blue, surging to his feet. She followed hurriedly, nearly tripping over an errant toolbox in her haste.

Blue's pulse thundered as she scrambled to gather their things, eager to escape before Jameson's companion emerged. Beside her, Ethan hastily shoved equipment into bags with quiet efficiency, his jaw clenched tight.

In her haste, Blue's foot collided with something solid wedged under the battered desk. She froze, eyes darting down instinctively. A slip of paper was just visible, tucked partway beneath what appeared to be a box of junk. Hardly daring to breathe, she slowly crouched down, straining to make out details in the gloom.

Gingerly pinching the paper between two fingers, she eased it free, her heart stuttering. Straightening up, she angled it toward the dim light filtering through cracks in the unit walls. It appeared to be some kind of receipt, columns of numbers marching down the page.

Before she could decipher more, Ethan grasped her shoulder urgently. "We've got to move, now," he whispered. "They could come back any second." Scooping up the last of their gear, he took her arm and guided her swiftly toward the exit.

Reaching the door first, Ethan paused, head cocked, listening intently. While he listened, Blue used a touch of magic to unlock the door, so they could escape. Detecting no sounds outside, he carefully pushed it upward, just enough for them to slip out into the rapidly fading twilight.

The hinges creaked faintly despite Ethan's delicate touch. Blue cringed, frozen halfway through the gap, the paper crumpled tightly in her fist. An agonizing few seconds passed before Ethan gestured hurriedly for her to follow.

They hurried through the maze of units toward Blue's waiting car, sticking to the shadows. Blue's nerves sang with tension, her eyes darting around for any sign of Jameson's crony. But the facility appeared deserted, only distant traffic sounds breaking the silence.

After what felt like an endless trek, they finally reached the parked car. Blue's sigh of relief emerged shaky and distorted as she slid inside, Ethan close behind. He stowed their gear and she started the engine, resisting the urge to peel out in her haste to flee the scene.

Only once the glow of the storage facility had faded in the rearview mirror did Blue feel her galloping heart begin to settle. Beside her, Ethan ran both hands roughly through his disheveled auburn hair, blowing out a long breath.

"That was too close," he muttered, shaking his head. "We need to lie low for a while, let things cool down before making another move."

Blue's fingers twitched toward the crumpled paper still clutched in her fist. "We may have already found our next move," she replied. Holding the page up to catch the last of the fading light, she scrutinized it again but the words remained indecipherable.

"It's some kind of receipt that was hidden under the desk," she explained. "I couldn't read what it says, but it could be important."

Ethan nodded slowly. "Could be a record of another shady deal. Or something placing him at the crime scene." He drummed his fingers on his thigh, gaze distant. "Whatever it is, we need to figure it out fast, before Jameson tries to cover his tracks permanently."

Chapter Thirteen

The comforting scent of chamomile tea steeped in the air
as Blue silently filled two faded mugs. She watched the
tendrils of steam rise and dissipate, finding the familiar
ritual soothing amidst the chaotic events of the evening.
Across the candy shop's cozy kitchen, Ethan leaned
against the counter, arms crossed over his broad chest. His
classically handsome features were creased in a thoughtful
frown, eyes distant and troubled.

Neither had spoken since collapsing breathlessly into the
sanctuary of the quiet shop after their near-miss at the
storage facility. Blue's mind was still spinning as she
replayed those tense, terrifying moments crouched behind
the dusty sofa. Her nerves hadn't stopped humming since
their narrow escape.

Almost against her will, her fingers drifted toward her
pocket, brushing the edge of the crumpled receipt stashed
within. The tantalizing scrap of paper called to her, urging
her to again unfold its cryptic contents. She clenched her
fist, resisting the urge. Not yet.

Picking up the mugs, she crossed to Ethan and offered
him one. He accepted it with a nod of thanks, the ceramic
dwarfed comically in his large palm. Blue leaned back
against the counter beside him, cradling her own mug
close to her chest and letting the warmth seep into her
still-chilled bones.

For long moments, the only sounds were the soothing tick of a wall clock and the gentle slosh as Ethan sipped his tea. Steam wreathed his rugged face, momentarily obscuring his pensive expression. Blue took a careful swallow of the scalding liquid, feeling it slide down her throat and blossom into a comforting heat in her core.

Unable to bear the suspense any longer, Blue set her mug down with a decisive clink. Ethan glanced up, one eyebrow raised. Keeping her eyes on the swirling amber contents of her cup, Blue reached into her pocket and withdrew the crumpled receipt. Smoothing it flat atop the counter, she felt Ethan lean closer with interest.

"I almost forgot about this, with everything else going on," Blue admitted. "But it could be important." She nudged the receipt closer to the overhead light, the better to make out the cramped columns of numbers.

Ethan's brow furrowed as he scrutinized the inscrutable figures. "What is it, some kind of code?"

"It looks more like a standard receipt to me," Blue mused. She lifted it, angling it under the bright light. "See there? That's a date at the very top."

She tapped it with one finger. "And it's marked the same night Tom was...the night he was killed." She swallowed hard, the words still difficult to utter aloud.

Ethan's dark eyebrows shot upward. "The night of? Well that's one hell of a coincidence. Any indication where it's from?" He leaned one palm on the counter as he peered closely at the tiny text.

"There's a shop name printed at the bottom - Lou's Sandwich Shop." Blue's eyes widened as recognition hit. "Wait. That place is only two blocks from where Tom's body was found."

Ethan let out a low whistle. "I'll be damned. That's quite the convenient alibi." His gaze found the customer name Blue indicated. "And this definitely says Derek Jameson here. Our elusive detective friend."

Blue's shoulders slumped as the implications sank in. "I thought this was finally the evidence we needed against him. But if he has proof he was somewhere else when it happened..." She crossed her arms with a huff of frustration.

Ethan held up a hand. "Now hold on, let's not get ahead of ourselves here. We don't know for sure yet if this clears him completely." He began to pace, a nervous habit when he was deep in thought. "For all we know, Jameson got takeout food that night to establish an alibi just in case."

Blue chewed her lower lip anxiously. "Maybe, but this seems pretty ironclad. Short of an eyewitness who can definitively place him at the scene, this could give him an airtight excuse."

"Possibly," Ethan conceded. "But it's suspicious enough to warrant looking into further. We should talk to the shop owner, jog his memory about that particular night. See if he distinctly remembers Jameson coming in."

He came to a stop, palms braced on the back of a cafe chair as he met her gaze. "If the owner confirms it, we'll have to rethink our approach. But I don't want to jump to any conclusions just yet."

Blue summoned a faint smile in response. "You're right, we should stay objective. It's just hard when it feels like we keep coming up against dead ends." She worried a hangnail on her thumb, a nervous habit from childhood.

Ethan crossed back to her and clasped her shoulder firmly. "I know it's frustrating. But we're making progress, even if it feels slow. This receipt may not be the smoking gun we wanted, but it's still a vital clue."

Reassured by his steady confidence, Blue took a deep breath and gathered her unraveling composure. "So what now?"

Ethan glanced at his watch, blinking blearily at the time. "Now, we both need some rest. It's nearly midnight, and we won't accomplish anything more tonight with exhausted brains."

He gently extracted the receipt from her reluctant fingers. "Get some sleep, Blue. We'll pay a visit to this sandwich shop first thing in the morning and hopefully get some answers."

Blue stifled a yawn, the late hour settling over her like a heavy blanket. Across the dimly lit kitchen, Ethan didn't look much more awake, rubbing his eyes blearily.

"We should talk this through before calling it a night," Blue said, nodding at the receipt lying between them.

Ethan blinked himself more alert. "Right, good idea to review where things stand." He picked up the receipt, angling it toward the light.

"So this puts Jameson near the crime scene on the night of the murder," he mused. "If he was at this Lou's Sandwich Shop when it happened, it gives him a potential alibi."

Blue worried her lip between her teeth. "A pretty strong one, unless we can definitively place him at the scene somehow."

"Very true," Ethan conceded. He tapped the receipt pensively. "We can't say for sure it clears him until we confirm the alibi's legitimacy."

"So what should our next move be?" Blue asked, stifling another yawn. The adrenaline crash was hitting hard.

"First, you need some rest," Ethan said with a gentle smile. "But then, I think we pay a visit to this sandwich shop, talk to the owner about that specific night. See if he distinctly remembers Jameson being there."

Blue nodded, feeling a bit more hopeful. "Okay, that's a good next step. We shouldn't assume this alibi is airtight yet."

"Exactly." Ethan pocketed the receipt securely. "Let's regroup refreshed in the morning and look into it further. I'm not ready to cross Jameson off the suspect list quite yet."

Blue smiled tiredly, comforted by his determination. She knew sleep would refresh her optimism and focus. There were still avenues left to pursue, and she wouldn't rest until Tom's case was solved.

***

The cheerfully bustling atmosphere of the sandwich shop enveloped Blue and Ethan as they stepped inside the next morning. Behind the counter, a jovial, rotund man deftly assembled an impressive stack of pastrami on rye. Glancing up at the door chime, he called over his shoulder, "Take a seat anywhere folks, I'll be right with ya!"

Settling into a vinyl booth by the window, Blue tried not to fidget with nervous anticipation. Before long, the man came sauntering over, wiping his hands on his apron. His name tag identified him as Lou, owner and proprietor.

"What can I get started for you two?" he asked congenially. Up close, his bushy gray mustache and laughing eyes gave him a kindly appearance.

Ethan flashed a polite smile. "We'll take two of your famous pastrami sandwiches. But first, if you have a moment, we wanted to ask you about a particular night last week."

Lou raised his eyebrows in interest. "Shoot, I'll try my best to remember."

Exchanging a quick glance with Blue, Ethan continued. "We're trying to confirm if a man named Derek Jameson was here on the evening of the seventeenth. We'd be grateful if you can recall."

Stroking his mustache thoughtfully, Lou stared into the distance for a long moment before snapping his fingers. "You know, I do remember that fella. Real twitchy, kept looking over his shoulder."

Blue and Ethan shared a surprised look. "So he was definitely here that specific night?" Ethan pressed.

"No doubt about it," Lou affirmed. "He came in right before closing, made a huge to-go order. I remember because it was a pain prepping that big of a meal when I was trying to shut the kitchen down."

"You're certain it was that day?" Blue asked.

Lou chuckled. "Absolutely sure. See, two of my best employees had called in sick. Some twenty-four-hour flu bug going around. So it was just me working that shift."

He gestured around the busy shop. "Not the easiest task, running this whole place solo. So that big order right before closing stood out for sure."

Ethan and Blue exchanged a disappointed look. His story seemed to verify Jameson's alibi beyond question.

Oblivious, Lou went on. "Yep, Jameson came in looking real anxious. Kept checking over his shoulder, you know? Seemed like he was in a big hurry too, even though he ordered half the menu."

He laughed heartily before his expression turned somber. "Funny enough, that was the same night that poor fella was found murdered over on Chestnut Street. Awful

141

business, that." Shaking his head sadly, he ambled off to put in their food order.

Blue slumped back in the vinyl booth, deflated. "I guess that's pretty definitive confirmation," she sighed, her last hopes fading.

Ethan nodded reluctantly. "Hard to argue with that level of detail. Sounds like an airtight alibi to me." Seeing her dejected face, he reached over and gave her hand an encouraging squeeze.

"But like I said last night, this doesn't completely exonerate him. He's guilty of something, even if it's not this specific murder," Ethan reminded gently. "We'll keep digging into his other shady activities and connections."

Blue offered a half-hearted smile in response. "You're right. And we'll keep pursuing every angle of Tom's case too. I'm not ready to give up yet."

She straightened up in her seat, renewed resolve pushing back her disappointment. Lou returned with their sandwiches, the mouthwatering smell lifting Blue's spirits slightly.

As they ate, Ethan appeared lost in thought, his brow creased. Swallowing a bite, he finally spoke. "You know, there's something that still doesn't add up to me."

Blue tilted her head curiously. "What's that?"

"The storage unit," Ethan mused after taking a sip of coffee. "It doesn't totally make sense that Jameson would keep all that incriminating evidence about his past dealings with Tom stashed away. If he really wanted to distance himself, why hang onto it all?"

Blue sat back, intrigued by this new angle. "You're absolutely right, it is odd. What are you thinking?"

"Well, the unit was newly rented," Ethan said. "What if Jameson found that stash of evidence somewhere else first? Somewhere connected to Tom himself?"

Blue's eyes widened, possibilities spinning open. "That's brilliant. Tom must have kept those items to use as blackmail or leverage." She leaned forward excitedly. "If we can figure out where Jameson found that evidence originally..."

"It could lead us to more clues about Tom's murder," Ethan finished. Their eyes locked, fresh hope blooming. This new avenue could be exactly the breakthrough they needed.

After leaving the sandwich shop, Blue turned to Ethan. "We need to go speak to Jameson directly. It's the only way we'll get answers now."

Ethan nodded, his jaw set grimly. "I agree. A direct confrontation is our only option at this point."

As they walked briskly down the sidewalk, Blue's mind raced as she tried to strategize. "We'll have to catch him off guard, apply some pressure. He won't give up the truth easily."

"No doubt about that," Ethan concurred. He rubbed his chin thoughtfully. "We'll have to come on strong, make it clear we aren't leaving without answers. But also avoid putting him so far on the defensive that he shuts down completely."

Blue chewed her lip, considering their limited options. "You're right, it will be a delicate balance. But we can do this." She met Ethan's gaze with fiery determination. "Let's go have a chat with Mr. Jameson."

Chapter Fourteen

The flickering red "Vacancy" sign provided the only illumination in the otherwise pitch-black parking lot. As Blue peered anxiously at the crumbling motel facade, she wondered if they had the right location. This ramshackle establishment didn't seem like somewhere a man of Jameson's means would choose to hide out.

She double-checked the address scrawled on the crumpled note in her palm. "Are we sure this is it?" she asked uncertainly.

Ethan nodded, his eyes scanning the rows of identical metal doors. "Positive. This is where my source indicated we'd find him."

Squaring her shoulders determinedly, Blue marched up to room 12 and rapped her knuckles sharply on the scarred wooden door. No answer came from within the dark room. She knocked again, harder this time. "Jameson!" she called out. "We know you're in there!"

Only ominous silence greeted her words. She huffed in growing frustration, casting an irritated glance at Ethan. He stepped forward and pounded his fist on the door so forcefully it rattled on its hinges.

"Open up, Jameson!" he bellowed. "We're not going anywhere until you talk to us!"

Finally, the door inched open a few feet, halted by a chain. One bloodshot eye peered out from the shadowy room beyond. Even in the dimness, Blue could tell the man was not Jameson.

Before he could react, Ethan slammed his palm against the door, breaking the flimsy chain and sending the stranger stumbling back. Storming over the threshold after him, Ethan grabbed two fistfuls of the man's shirt.

"Where the hell is Jameson?" he thundered.

The disheveled young man stumbled back, thrown off balance by Ethan's aggressive entrance. His eyes were wide with shock and alarm at the strangers now invading his motel room.

Sensing an opportunity in the man's obvious intimidation, Blue swiftly moved to block any escape route to the door or bathroom. Her usually kind eyes were steely with determination.

Ethan advanced until he had the smaller man cornered. "Where is Derek Jameson?" he demanded. When no reply came, he slammed his palm against the wall just inches from the man's head. "I won't ask again!"

The man flinched, throwing up his hands defensively. "I don't know any Jameson!" His voice quavered with fear.

Exchanging a knowing look with Blue, Ethan grabbed two fistfuls of the man's shirt and shoved him forcefully against the wall. "That's BS and we both know it," Ethan growled. "You're going to tell me everything you know about Derek Jameson's involvement in Tom Wiseman's murder."

The man's eyes bugged. "Murder? I don't know what you're talking about, I swear!" He struggled in vain to break Ethan's viselike grip.

Sensing he required more convincing, Ethan tightened his hold and got directly in the man's face. "Quit playing dumb. You know exactly why we're here." He enunciated each word deliberately. "Where. Is. Derek. Hiding. The evidence?"

The man's breath came in panicked gasps, his face reddening. Finally, he choked out, "Okay, okay! I'll tell you whatever you want, just please let me go!"

Ethan immediately released him, taking a step back and crossing his arms expectantly. The man sagged back against the wall, rubbing his throat. After taking a moment to catch his breath, he finally met Ethan's flinty stare.

"I'm Eli," he mumbled, defeat in his tone. "Derek Jameson is my brother."

Blue felt a flare of vindication. They had correctly guessed this man's connection. Stepping forward but keeping her distance, she addressed him calmly but firmly.

"Eli, we need you to tell us where Derek is and what he told you about the evidence he found related to Tom Wiseman's murder." She held his wavering gaze. "Don't try to protect him. We know he's guilty and you're our only chance at getting justice for Tom."

Eli's shoulders slumped. He studied the stained carpet intently before finally responding. "Derek didn't kill Tom,"

147

he said softly. "But they had a...a business dispute. It ended badly."

Trapped against the dingy wallpaper, Eli's eyes darted wildly like a cornered animal. Ethan loomed over him, muscular arms crossed over his broad chest. His expression was hard, unrelenting.

"We're not leaving until you tell us everything you know," Ethan stated, his deep voice rumbling with authority. "What is Derek's connection to Tom Wiseman's murder?"

Eli's throat bobbed as he swallowed nervously. "I already told you, I don't know anything about a murder!" Despite his defiant words, his wavering tone betrayed the lie. Sweat beaded his pale forehead under Ethan's intense scrutiny.

Unmoved, Ethan pressed closer, using his imposing physical presence to full intimidating effect. "You can't protect your brother anymore. Tell us where to find the evidence he took from Tom's place."

Cornered and fearful, Eli searched desperately for an escape but found none. His thin shoulders finally slumped in defeat. When he spoke, his voice was scarcely a whisper.

"Derek's been looking for evidence Tom had against him. If it got out, it would ruin his life." Eli nervously wet his lips before continuing. "They found it in Tom's garage. Broke in the night of his viewing before the funeral."

Ethan's eyes gleamed, sensing triumph close at hand. Maintaining his stance crowding Eli, he crossed his arms expectantly. "Go on. Tell us everything."

Visibly cracking under the pressure, Eli spilled out the rest in a rush. "It was stuff Tom had collected to blackmail Derek from their old business dealings. He doctored records to make Derek take the fall if anything went wrong. Derek just wanted to find it before the truth came out."

Eli slumped back against the faded wallpaper, the fight draining from his body. His fingers pulled at loose threads on his shirt hem as he avoided Ethan's piercing gaze. After an uncomfortable stretch of silence, Ethan prompted gruffly, "There's more you're not telling us. Keep talking."

With a resigned sigh, Eli reluctantly continued his confession. "We thought we had plenty of time to search the garage thoroughly. Tom's funeral was the next morning." He worried his lower lip before going on.

"But Margery - Tom's wife - she showed up right after we broke in. I thought for sure we were done for." Eli shook his head, as if still in disbelief. "But when she realized what we were doing, she just stood there watching us."

Brow furrowed, Ethan leaned forward intently. "She caught you red-handed and just let you keep searching?" Skepticism colored his tone.

Eli nodded, blinking rapidly. "I was shocked too. She didn't yell at us to leave or call the cops. She just said..." He paused, seeming to replay the interaction in his mind. "She just said to take anything relevant so she wouldn't have to deal with it."

He gave a baffled shrug. "After that, she walked out without another word. We found what we needed and got out of there fast. Didn't question our luck, you know?"

Ethan stroked his stubbled chin thoughtfully. This new information opened up further questions. What was Margery's motive for permitting the break-in? Did she simply want to wash her hands of the situation, or was there more to it?

Sensing Eli had revealed all he knew for now, Ethan backed toward the door. They'd gotten plenty to pursue for the time being. "We'll be in touch if we have further questions," he stated gruffly.

Leaving Eli slumped dejectedly on the sagging mattress, Ethan exited the motel room with Blue close on his heels. They had made huge strides today thanks to Eli's coerced confession.

Blue stepped out of the cramped, musty motel room into the biting chill of the night, a welcome contrast to the stale air she'd been breathing. She took deep, cleansing breaths, the cold air filling her lungs and clearing her head. With a sense of relief, she made her way to the car, its engine humming softly in the quiet night, a beacon of warmth in the frosty air.

Ethan, already inside, turned the heat up as Blue slid into the passenger seat, her body immediately beginning to shiver in response to the sudden change in temperature. "It's absolutely freezing out there," she exclaimed, rubbing her hands together for warmth. "I'm really looking forward to getting back home and defrosting a bit."

Ethan put the car into gear, pulling smoothly out of the motel parking lot. "Before we head back, we should grab something to eat," he suggested. "Planning our next move, especially that interrogation, is going to require some serious energy."

Despite the late hour, they decided on a nearby diner that was open around the clock. The place had a welcoming glow, its lights a soft beacon in the dark night. They slid into a booth upholstered in cracked vinyl, the menus in front of them a promise of much-needed sustenance. It was only then that Blue realized how hungry she was; the day's stress and constant adrenaline had pushed her appetite to the back of her mind, but now it roared to the forefront.

They ordered generously, the comfort food a perfect antidote to the day's tensions. As they waited for their meal, Ethan looked at Blue thoughtfully. "We need to talk about Margery and her potential motives," he said, his expression serious.

Blue took a bite of her burger, considering his words. "When Margery came into the shop before, she seemed really upset about Tom's affair," she recalled. "But there was also this sense of... relief, maybe? That he was out of the picture."

Ethan nodded, remembering the details Blue had shared earlier. "You mentioned she was pretty worked up about that custom candy order for Tom's mistress. She definitely wasn't happy about the cheating."

"Right," Blue agreed, taking a sip of her coffee. "So, could her giving Derek and Eli access be some sort of revenge against Tom?"

Ethan tilted his head, looking skeptical. "It's possible, but it feels like a bit of a leap. Being upset about an affair is one thing, but helping to undermine a police investigation is another level entirely."

Blue frowned, playing with her fries. "Yeah, you're probably right. There's got to be something more personal, more compelling driving her actions."

Ethan refilled their coffee mugs from the carafe on the table. "I think our visit tomorrow will shed a lot of light on this," he said confidently. "We'll get the full story, straight from Margery herself."

Chapter Fifteen

Blue hummed to herself as she stood in front of the bathroom mirror, carefully applying mascara. She had a big day ahead, with plans to finally confront Margery, and wanted to look put together and professional.

As she set the mascara wand down, a sleek black figure leapt onto the counter, nearly knocking over various bottles. "Like, can we go to the mall today?" Tiffany asked, swishing her tail impatiently. "I'm meeting Brenda at 11:00."

With a tired sigh, Blue recapped the mascara and reminded the stubborn familiar, "Tiffany, how many times do I have to explain this? Brenda is a fictional character from an old TV show. She's not real. Please stop asking to go to the mall to meet your imaginary friend."

Tiffany huffed, offended. "Brenda is my bestie! Just because you have no social life doesn't mean you can, like, ruin mine."

Before Blue could respond, footsteps sounded down the hall, followed by Pepper breezing into the bathroom. "Ooh, are we going shopping?" she asked eagerly.

"Absolutely not," Blue replied. "Tiffany is pestering me to go to the mall again for some delusional reason."

Flicking her tail disdainfully, Tiffany retorted, "I just wanted a new makeover look for summer! But clearly you fashion- challenged losers can't make that dream come true."

Pepper and Blue exchanged an amused look. "Is that all?" Pepper said. "If Tiffany wants a makeover, I think we can handle that right here!"

Despite Tiffany's spluttering protests, the two enthusiastic sisters whisked her into the adjoining bedroom. Blue rummaged in the closet and unearthed a forgotten pink rhinestone cat sweater.

"How cute is this?" she exclaimed, even as Tiffany yowled in horror. Before she could escape, Blue had wrestled her into the frilly outfit.

"Adorable!" Pepper pronounced. "But it needs some accessories." She grabbed a feather boa and dramatically draped it around Tiffany's neck.

"Absolutely not!" Tiffany huffed. "I look like a clown! A fashionable cat would never!" But her complaints went ignored.

Next came a sparkly bow collar clipped into place. Then Pepper gleefully added the pièce de résistance - a thorough coating of shimmery purple body glitter combed through Tiffany's sleek fur.

"Now for the finishing touch!" Pepper quickly sculpted Tiffany's headfur into an impressive faux-hawk style held in place with kitty-safe hair gel. Stepping back, the sisters admired their work.

"You look utterly fabulous!" Blue declared as Tiffany craned her neck trying to see the outrageous style. "Are you happy now? You finally got your makeover."

Tiffany turned up her nose disdainfully. "This is, like, the most heinous thing I've ever seen. My stylist at the Pawlor would be appalled." But despite her haughty words, Blue detected a hint of delight sparking in her eyes.

"Say cheese!" Pepper suddenly cried, whipping out her phone. Before Tiffany could protest, she began snapping photos from every angle, determined to capture the memorable look.

"Stop, I'm so embarrassed!" Tiffany wailed half-heartedly. But she soon began primping and posing with exaggerated flair. The sisters exchanged a knowing grin - their diva kitty was secretly loving the attention.

For nearly a half hour, an impromptu photo shoot unfolded. Tiffany grew increasingly into her model role, prancing and preening for each shot. Blue and Pepper could barely contain their laughter at her exaggerated expressions and poses.

When Tiffany finally collapsed in happy exhaustion, Pepper uploaded the entire sparkly portfolio to her Insta. "Now you have an amazing magazine spread to remember your makeover by," she said with a smile.

Despite some lingering grumbles about the indignity, a purring Tiffany butted her glittery head against the sisters affectionately. "I guess you peasants managed an adequate look this time," she conceded. "But next time, we're totes going to a real stylist! This makeover was almost tragic, but I made it work because I'm so glam. But gag me with a spoon before I let you amateurs style me again!"

She flicked her tail sassily before adding, "I'm fierce no matter what, but we need to take my look to the next level. I'm thinking highlights, extensions, the works! We'll make it a girls' day and hit up the Pawlor. It will be totally stellar!"

Rolling their eyes good-naturedly, Blue and Pepper simply enjoyed having lighthearted fun together. For a brief time, their worries faded away, replaced by playful family bonding.

Tiffany leapt onto Blue's quilt-covered bed with a dramatic flop, letting out an exaggerated yawn. "OMG, that makeover was totes exhausting! This kitty desperately needs her beauty rest." She turned in lazy circles, the bedsprings squeaking beneath her, before curling up atop the pile of plush pillows.

Within seconds, she was snoring softly, her sides rising and falling rhythmically. Blue and Pepper exchanged an amused grin at the diva familiar's antics. Tiffany could never pass up an opportunity to be over-the-top.

Leaving her to nap, the sisters tiptoed down to the cozy kitchen. Slanting rays of morning sun shone through the blue gingham curtains covering the window over the sink.

"I'm starving after all that excitement," Pepper declared, peering into the fridge. "What do we have for breakfast?"

Rifling through the freezer, Blue found an unopened box of toaster waffles buried behind a carton of unopened sugar-free ice cream. She briefly wondered how that got there... because who on earth would buy that stuff... "How do waffles sound? I can cook up the last of the bacon too."

"Ooh, yes, please!" Pepper readily agreed to the sweet and salty combo. She plopped her bulging bookbag onto the round wooden table and began digging through its contents while Blue got cooking.

Soon the toaster ejected two crisp, golden squares while the microwave sputtered and sizzled as it crisped the bacon. Blue expertly maneuvered around Pepper, who was engrossed in sorting through her mess of school supplies and papers strewn across the tabletop.

"Berry jam or regular maple syrup?" Blue asked, holding up two condiment bottles.

"Both!" Pepper responded enthusiastically. True to her sweet tooth, she liked mixing flavors.

Chuckling indulgently, Blue smothered the waffles liberally in syrup and jam before depositing the heaping plates on the table. The rich, welcoming smells made both their mouths water.

As Blue carried over mugs of fresh coffee, Pepper surreptitiously slid an official-looking piece of paper under her folder. "So, uh, I need you to sign something," she said lightly, avoiding eye contact. "Just pen to paper, no biggie."

Curious, Blue picked it up and saw 'Midterm Report Card' printed boldly across the top. "Wait, we're getting midterm reports now?" she asked in surprise. That was new.

"Yeah, school board decided it would, uh, help keep parents more informed," Pepper mumbled through a mouthful of waffle.

Scanning the page, Blue saw mostly As and Bs reflected Pepper's normally solid academic performance. But two grades in particular caught her eye - a D in chemistry and an F in gym class.

Raising an eyebrow, she met Pepper's studiously averted gaze. "Pepper, want to tell me what's going on with these two grades?" she gently prompted.

Cheeks reddening, Pepper toyed with her napkin and explained she was struggling with her chem lessons lately. "But it's okay, I already set up mandatory study sessions with a tutor to get caught up," she added reassuringly.

Blue nodded, relieved Pepper was being proactive. "I'm glad you took the initiative to get help. In the future please come to me sooner if you're having trouble in a class."

"I know, I'm sorry," Pepper said sheepishly before quickly pivoting topics. "But gym is a lost cause. I'm just going for a passing D, honestly. That class is totally pointless anyw—"

"Ah-ah," Blue gently interrupted. "I know you dislike gym, but you do need to pass it to graduate. Let's aim for that minimum passing grade, okay? I don't expect straight As, just put in the bare effort you need."

"Ugh, fine," Pepper sighed dramatically, though she seemed relieved by Blue's calm reaction.

Dutifully, she grabbed the pen and handed it to Blue. Once her sister had signed on the "Guardian Signature" line, she signed the report card where indicated for "Student" before tucking it safely back into her folder.

An easy, lighthearted chatter filled the sunny kitchen as the two sisters finished their leisurely breakfast. Pepper entertained Blue with amusing school gossip while Blue refilled their mugs. It was a nice moment of normalcy.

As Pepper gathered her things to leave, she offhandedly mentioned, "Oh, by the way, I'm catching a ride today instead of the bus."

Blue paused, turning from the sink with a surprised look. "A ride? With whom?" As far as she knew, none of Pepper's friends had their licenses yet.

"Just someone I met recently," Pepper replied vaguely, already edging toward the front door. "I'll tell you more about them soon! If I decide he's worth it."

"Wait! He?!?" Blue called, but the door was already swinging shut behind Pepper's beat-up Chucks. Distractedly drying her hands on a dish towel, Blue tried not to fret over this new development. But she resolved to gently press Pepper for more details about this mysterious new companion soon. For now, she'd let it go and hope it was an innocuous schoolfriend.

With the kitchen tidied up, she headed to the bedroom to grab her purse. But despite the comforting familiarity of their home, Blue's thoughts kept returning to the unknown person whisking her teenage sister around. She wanted to respect Pepper's independence, but her protective instincts were on high alert.

The aroma of freshly brewed coffee permeated the air as Blue tidied up the kitchen after breakfast. She hummed softly to herself, looking forward to getting to the candy shop to meet Ethan and finally confronting Margery. A knock at the front door interrupted her musings.

Padding down the hallway, she peered through the eyehole to see Brock's familiar face. That was odd - he usually called or texted before stopping by. Swinging open the door, she greeted him with a quizzical smile.

"Hey, Brock, what brings you..." She trailed off as she registered his grim expression, the forced smile sliding off her face. "Is everything okay?"

Brock shifted his weight, glancing past her into the house. "Mind if I come in for a minute? We should talk."

"Uh, sure." Blue stepped aside, bewilderment growing as he brushed past her without another word. She followed him down the hall to the warmly lit kitchen.

"Can I get you some coffee?" she offered reflexively. Without waiting for an answer, she grabbed two mugs and filled them from the still warm pot.

Brock accepted his silently, taking a seat at the round wooden table. The normalcy of his favorite Superman mug contrasted oddly with the tension radiating off him in waves. Blue sat across from him, gripping her mug tightly.

"So..." she ventured hesitantly after an awkward beat, "to what do I owe the pleasure of your company this morning? Are you here to arrest me?"

Brock didn't crack a smile, his mouth set in a thin line.

"Wait, are you?"

He took a bracing gulp of coffee before replying. "Nothing like that. I wanted to discuss the other night, when you...had company stay over."

Blue's eyes widened, nearly sloshing her coffee. "Company? What are you..." Comprehension dawned and she slammed her mug down. "How do you know about that? Have you been spying on me?"

"Don't be absurd," Brock huffed, though his ears reddened slightly. "Besides, Blue, we've been friends since forever. If I had, I would call it checking up on you, not spying. But I heard it from Pepper. Ran into her at school yesterday."

Fighting to control her indignation, Blue bit out, "Oh, so now you're just 'running into' my teenage sister to grill her about my personal life?"

Brock held up a hand placatingly. "Now hold on, that's not what happened. I was there handling an incident and saw Pepper when classes let out for lunch. She's the one who happened to mention your guest in conversation."

Leaning back and crossing her arms, Blue asked pointedly, "And what official police business did the undersheriff possibly have at a high school?"

Brock shifted in his seat, avoiding her skeptical stare. "Just some contraband confiscated, nothing you need to worry about," he said evasively. "The point is—"

"The point," Blue interrupted testily, "is you seem awfully interested in my personal affairs lately. Spying, stalking, interrogating my sister..."

"No one's been spying!" Brock snapped, smacking his palm on the table in frustration. "I'm just concerned. Letting some strange man spend the night was reckless, Blue."

Shoving back her chair, Blue stood and began angrily clearing their half-finished coffees. "First of all, Ethan was just being considerate because I wasn't feeling well. And secondly, it's none of your damn business!"

She slammed the mugs into the sink, coffee sloshing over the rim. Gripping the counter, she took a deep breath before turning to face him again. "I don't know what Pepper told you, but she wasn't in any danger. So you can stop the overbearing routine."

Rising slowly, Brock looked vaguely wounded by her words. "I apologize, I didn't intend to overstep. I only brought it up because I care about you and Pepper." He closed the distance between them, voice softening. "I just want you both to be safe."

Some of Blue's anger dissipated at the sincerity in his eyes. She knew his protectiveness came from a place of genuine care. With a small sigh, she said more gently, "We were perfectly safe, I promise. Ethan was a complete gentleman."

Brock still looked unconvinced. "Maybe so, but you barely know him. Men can seem harmless at first..." He trailed off with a weighted look.

Bristling again, Blue snapped, "Yes, I'm well aware men can be wolves in sheep's clothing." She turned her back on him, busying herself wiping the already clean counter.

"But I'm an excellent judge of character. And I wouldn't have allowed it if I sensed even a hint of ill intent from Ethan." She tossed the rag into the sink forcefully. "You know that my intuition is… almost supernatural."

Brock hovered uncertainly behind her. When she whirled to face him again, anger simmered in her eyes. "Quite frankly, I don't appreciate you insinuating I can't make sound decisions. Or that I would foolishly endanger my own sister."

Brock's shoulders were squared, his expression resolute. "I apologize for overstepping," he said firmly. "But you can't blame me for being concerned."

He moved toward the door but paused, turning back. "Just try not to let that man's giant biceps cloud your judgment." His face was impassive, but there was an edge to his voice.

Taken aback, Blue wondered if she detected a hint of jealousy in his parting words. Before she could respond, the door clicked decisively shut behind his retreating back.

Alone again, Blue bristled as irritation and guilt swirled within her. She knew Brock cared, but clearly he didn't fully trust her instincts. With a frustrated huff, she grabbed her things, thoughts consumed by the impending confrontation with Margery. At least that deceitful woman's judgment was rightfully suspect.

***

The late morning sun glinted off the sleek black exterior of Ethan's motorcycle as he pulled up outside Sucre Bleu. Blue waved from the shop door, locking it behind her before hurrying over to meet him.

"Ready for this?" Ethan asked, handing her a spare helmet. His eyes were alight beneath the visor of his own headgear.

Blue nodded firmly as she climbed on behind him, gripping his waist. "I've been ready for a long time. Let's go get some answers."

The engine roared to life beneath them as they sped off toward the affluent neighborhood where Margery resided. Blue clung to Ethan, the wind whipping around them. But her nerves were steady - she was prepared for the confrontation ahead.

Soon they rolled to a stop outside the imposing iron gates guarding Margery's sprawling home. Pressing the intercom, they stated their names and desire to speak with her regarding Tom's case. After a staticky pause, the gates swung slowly open.

As they walked the brick path leading to the formidable front door, Blue met Ethan's gaze with a silent nod.

Together, they would uncover whatever secrets lurked behind Margery's composed facade.

The door swung open before they could knock, Margery's flawlessly made-up face betraying no surprise at their arrival. "Please, come in," she greeted smoothly, ushering them down the hall toward a sitting room.

The space was meticulously decorated in shades of cream and gold, exuding wealth and privilege. Margery settled gracefully onto a velvet chaise lounge, gesturing for them to take the couch opposite her.

"To what do I owe the pleasure?" she asked lightly, as if their unannounced visit was a social call. Her cool gaze revealed nothing.

Blue dove right in, wasting no time on pleasantries. "We've learned some interesting things about the night your home was broken into, Margery," she began bluntly. "About your...lack of response."

Margery's smile remained fixed as if carved from marble. "Whatever do you mean?"

Leaning forward intently, Blue continued. "We know you caught Derek Jameson and his brother searching the garage. And you let them take evidence, including items stolen from a crime scene."

For the first time, Margery's composure seemed to crack. Her eyes narrowed almost imperceptibly. "You seem to be laboring under some false assumptions," she said, a note of steel entering her voice.

Ethan crossed his arms, gaze boring into her. "No assumptions. We have a solid confession. Care to explain why you allowed material related to your husband's murder to be taken?"

Margery stood abruptly, smoothing her skirt with a sharp motion. When she faced them again, her features were schooled into a mask of polite indifference.

"I think you should leave now," she stated evenly. But Blue and Ethan didn't budge.

Rising slowly, Blue kept her eyes locked on Margery's. "We know you wanted Tom exposed and humiliated. Was his death part of that plan too?"

Something seemed to shift in Margery's eyes at Blue's words. Her shoulders sank slightly as the mask of composure slipped. Moving to the window, she gazed out unseeingly.

"No," she said finally, her voice barely a whisper. "I didn't want him dead. Just...ruined. The way he ruined so many." She turned back, defiance mingling with grief on her face.

"After years of callous treatment, I needed to see him pay. To have his lies dragged into the light." She resumed her seat, gazing at Blue intently. "Can you understand that, at least?"

Studying Margery's defeated yet unrepentant expression, Blue felt a surprising pang of empathy. However misguided her actions, Margery was clearly a victim too.

Margery averted her gaze, appearing oddly vulnerable for the first time since their arrival. She sank gracefully back onto the velvet chaise, arranging her skirt with deliberate care.

Just as Blue opened her mouth to respond, Margery suddenly regained her composure. Leaning forward intently, her voice turned brisk and businesslike once more.

"While I understand your desire to find answers, you're wasting time pursuing me. I suggest speaking with that little harlot Sierra instead." Her lip curled derisively as she spoke the other woman's name.

Exchanging a glance with Ethan, Blue asked carefully, "What makes you think Sierra was involved? We know about the affair, yes, but nothing more than that."

Margery waved a hand dismissively. "Oh, please, it was more than just an affair. The woman was utterly obsessed, totally in love with my husband." Her tone dripped disgust and contempt.

"She had no shame pursuing a married man," Margery continued spitefully. "I knew about the sordid relationship for months. Hired a private investigator to uncover evidence against them both."

She paused, smoothing invisible wrinkles from her skirt. "Check her alibi, question her activities, turn up the heat. I suspect you'll find exactly what you're looking for." She smiled then, visibly pleased at the prospect.

A charged silence hung in the air after Margery's startling claims about Sierra. Blue's mind spun with questions, but it was clear the enigmatic woman had revealed all she intended to for now.

Rising gracefully from her chair, Margery clasped her hands. "Now, I must ask you both to be on your way. I'm expected at a luncheon." Her tone left no room for argument.

Blue and Ethan stood slowly, realizing they had been dismissed. But as Margery began ushering them briskly down the hall, Blue paused.

"One last thing. May we have a quick look in your garage before we go?" She kept her voice casual, as if the request was an afterthought. "I know the police have already searched it thoroughly, but fresh eyes sometimes help."

Margery's startled look confirmed she had hoped to avoid allowing them access. But painting on a polite smile, she acquiesced. "Of course, if you feel it's necessary."

Trying to hide their eagerness, Blue and Ethan followed her through the sprawling house to a set of French doors leading outside. Margery unlocked them with a key from a keyring she pulled from her pocket, ushering them into the cavernous space.

"I'm afraid you won't find anything new," she said airily. "As I mentioned, Derek and his brother were quite...thorough in their search."

Ignoring her, Blue and Ethan began meticulously scouring every inch of the garage. They searched behind tools, peered under tarps, and shifted boxes and furniture, seeking any clues the untrained Jameson brothers may have missed.

After nearly an hour of fruitless searching, frustration mounting, Blue rested her forehead against a storage shelf in defeat. She was about to suggest they move on when she noticed something peculiar.

The shelf seemed ever so slightly askew, its edges not aligning flush with the wall. Brow furrowing, Blue traced her fingers along the outside edge, finding a tiny gap. Gripping tightly, she gave an experimental tug.

To her astonishment, the entire shelf swung forward easily on concealed hinges, revealing a small hidden room behind the false wall.

Chapter Sixteen

Stepping further into the small, windowless room, Blue felt a chill run down her spine that had nothing to do with the temperature. The space was filled from floor to ceiling with an elaborate setup of monitors, servers, and electronics equipment. But most chilling was the implication of what they had found.

"He was spying on people," Ethan muttered in disbelief, voicing her own dawning realization. His gaze remained fixed on the towering racks of servers along one side of the room as he moved to examine them closer.

Blue's skin crawled at the thought. What kind of person would secretly invade the privacy of those around them on such a massive scale? It seemed Tom's immorality ran deeper than they could have guessed.

"Look here," Ethan called. He had opened a panel on one of the servers, revealing rows of neatly labeled hard drives. The labels made Blue's blood turn to ice - names of local townspeople and businesses she knew well.

Horrified, her fingers traced over the small white stickers marking each drive: Carson House. McKinley Residence. Lunatic Fringe Salon. And, with a jolt of outrage, Sucre Bleu Candy Shoppe.

"That snake," she choked out as the violation sank in. Not only had Tom spied on friends and neighbors, but he had also specifically targeted her beloved store. Who knew what private moments he had captured within her little sanctuary?

Ethan placed a bracing hand on her shoulder, his own jaw clenched with anger on her behalf. "Breathe, Blue. We're finally getting justice for what he did." His voice hardened as he continued. "Let's see what kind of evidence he kept on file."

Nodding stiffly, Blue realized Ethan was right - the answers were literally within her grasp now. She steeled herself and moved to the computer terminal, hitting the power button. As the monitors flickered to life, an eerie glow filled the dark room.

Then the home pages loaded, providing a directory to access the recorded footage for each location. Blue scrolled through rapidly, her unease growing as the list continued seemingly without end. Tom's twisted voyeurism clearly knew no bounds.

Selecting the folder simply labeled 'Residence', live feeds from multiple rooms of Tom's own home appeared. The opulent interiors were jarringly mundane as Blue skimmed through them, searching for any clue as to why he was surveilling his own property so extensively.

Then a flicker of movement on one feed caught her eye. Adjusting the camera angle, her breath caught in recognition. Displayed in full HD glory was Tom's bedroom, where a couple was enthusiastically entangled atop silken sheets.

"Is that...?" Ethan asked over her shoulder, equally startled. Blue just nodded, a blush rising on her cheeks. The amorous duo seemed oblivious to the prying camera lens, lost in their illicit passion.

Quickly exiting that feed, Blue continued flipping through the others. It was clear Tom's motivations went far beyond just security concerns. His arrogance in spying on his own infidelity was galling. What other sordid acts might they uncover in the hours of footage he had collected?

A growing sense of violated outrage fueled Blue as they scrutinized each drive's contents. She was more determined than ever to uncover the full truth of Tom's vile secrets and bring all his many victims the justice they deserved. The answers were here, just waiting to be brought into the light.

A heavy silence hung in the air as Blue and Ethan continued searching methodically through the vast trove of surveillance footage Tom had compiled. Each new discovery added to the growing portrait of a man corrupted by unchecked power and greed.

Seeing intimate moments of private lives play out made Blue's skin crawl with violation. It was a gross ethical transgression, capturing people without consent or knowledge simply because you could.

But even more disturbing was the purpose behind the extensive spying. As they scrutinized footage, a pattern emerged of Tom leveraging what he captured for personal gain and control.

"Look at this," Ethan said grimly, cueing up a video dated a few months prior. It showed a local woman Blue recognized entering Tom's study, face streaked with tears. Tom sat smugly behind his desk, tossing a manila envelope down between them.

Though the footage had no audio, the woman's anguished expression made the nature of the meeting clear. With shaking hands she picked up the envelope—likely containing photos or evidence Tom was using against her. After a brief exchange, Tom ushered her out, looking satisfied.

"He was blackmailing her," Blue said in disgust. "Abusing his power to extort and manipulate people." She thought of the violation that woman must have felt, her life forever marred.

They uncovered several more such instances of Tom ruthlessly exploiting what his spying yielded. In each video, his smug smile and domineering presence made Blue's blood boil with loathing.

But worse was his evident feeling of invincibility in recording his own crimes. As the tapes revealed him growing more overtly threatening when demands weren't met, she realized his arrogance had no limit.

"He kept evidence that could destroy him because he didn't think he could be touched," Ethan said, echoing Blue's thoughts. "He probably got a thrill out of documenting it all."

Blue's hands curled into fists, nails biting into her palms. Amidst the hours of illicit footage, one particular group of files caught Blue's eye - a folder simply labeled "Malone." She clicked it open hesitantly, stomach knotting with dread at what fresh violation she might uncover.

As the most recent video loaded, a familiar facade came into view on the screen - the modest two-story home of Jack Malone, who lived just down the street from Tom's lavish residence. Blue instantly recalled Jack mentioning Tom's unrelenting harassment, though the true extent of it was only now being revealed.

At first, the camera angle provided an innocuous glimpse of Jack's front walk. But as she scrolled through the trove of tapes, an increasingly unsettling portrait emerged.

Tom had catalogued countless hours of Jack going about mundane daily activities - getting the mail, leaving for work, washing his car in the driveway. It was a gross invasion of privacy, but it seemed relatively harmless at first.

However, as she delved deeper, the footage took a more sinister turn. Hidden cameras inside Jack's home displayed private arguments with his wife, vulnerable moments alone.

Blue's stomach churned with indignation. It was a shocking betrayal, to feel safe in your own space without realizing you were being watched intimately in your most private, unfiltered moments.

Worst of all was footage revealing Tom himself trespassing on Jack's property to inflict gradual torments designed to fray his mental state. Ripping flowerbeds, scratching his car, clogging drains to flood the basement – petty but maddening acts.

Through it all, Tom's smug grin gleamed with twisted pleasure at exerting control and slowly dismantling Jack's peace of mind. Blue seethed at this abuse of power, the cruelty of using what should have been harmless technology to systematically torment another human being.

Blue forced herself to continue systematically reviewing tapes of the suspects, trying to tune out the churning unease at witnessing such intimate violations of privacy. Just when the fruitless watching threatened to overwhelm her, something stopped her cold.

"Oh my god," she choked out, hand flying to her mouth. Heart hammering, she froze the frame, rewound five seconds, and played it again, certain she had misseen it. But there was no mistake.

She turned to Ethan, eyes wide with shock. "I don't believe it," she whispered.

Chapter Seventeen

Blue's stomach dropped as a familiar setting flickered across the screen – the cozy confines of her kitchen at Sucre Bleu. She would recognize the lovingly painted robin's egg blue cabinets and hanging copper pots anywhere.

Revulsion crept through her as she realized Tom had violated the sanctuary of her shop too. She watched with growing unease as the Blue on tape cheerfully whirled around the kitchen, oblivious to the prying camera.

At first, it seemed a mundane scene of her preparing batches of fudge and brittle for the shop. But as the minutes ticked by, Blue sensed something wasn't right. Her movements on screen became more fluid and hypnotic, her lips softly chanting indecipherable words.

Blue's heart seized in panic as she recognized what she was witnessing. The camera had captured her subtly performing magic, intended to infuse the candy with positive energy and good fortune for her customers.

"Oh, god," she whimpered, hands flying to cover her mouth in horror. Her most closely guarded secret, exposed to Tom's all-seeing lens. What if he had archived this footage elsewhere too? The implications were terrifying.

Ethan glanced over sharply, immediately concerned. "What's wrong? Did you notice something?" His brows were knitted with worry.

Blue's thoughts raced wildly, searching for a plausible explanation besides the truth. If Ethan knew, there was no telling how he would react or judge her. The risk was too great.

"I...I'm not really sure," she stammered unconvincingly. "It must be some kind of camera glitch or optical illusion." She forced an unnatural laugh. "Makes it look like I'm up to something strange, but I'm clearly just cooking."

Ethan's piercing blue eyes lingered on her face, his expression belying skepticism. "Are you sure? It seemed like..." He trailed off uncertainly.

Blue's pulse pounded as she silently pleaded for him to drop it. After an endless pause, he finally gave a short nod and turned back to the screens. "Yeah, must be some weird tech malfunction. Anyway, let's move on. There has to be a clue here somewhere."

Slumping back in her chair, Blue slowly released the breath she had been holding. Her secret was intact, but she had never felt more exposed and vulnerable. She couldn't risk letting her guard down again until every last second of Tom's invasive footage was permanently erased.

A tense beat of silence hung in the air before Ethan spoke again, his tone careful. "I have to ask...any idea why Tom was spying on your shop like this? Seems pretty invasive for no reason."

Blue's pulse spiked again at the question. She scrambled to concoct a plausible explanation, buying time by pretending to study her hands.

"Well, you know we didn't exactly get along," she began slowly. "Tom was never satisfied with my candy no matter what I did. I guess...I guess he disliked me enough that he wanted ammunition against me."

Ethan frowned. "What do you mean, ammunition?"

Blue gave a weak shrug, avoiding his probing gaze. "He was always convinced I was cutting corners, ignoring regulations. I'm sure he hoped hidden cameras would catch me doing something improper he could report."

She risked a glance at Ethan, holding her breath. His expression was a mix of disbelief and disgust. "Let me get this straight - he disliked your candy so much, he stalked and spied on you trying to get you shut down?"

Hating the deception but seeing no alternative, Blue nodded mutely.

Ethan sat back with a huff, shaking his head. "Unbelievable. But I suppose a guy warped enough to do all this—" he gestured at the screens "—would be capable of that too."

Blue managed a weak murmur of agreement, immensely relieved he had accepted the excuse. Anxious to change the subject, she quickly clicked on the next video file.

It was footage from inside a stately bedroom she didn't recognize at first. But as two figures fell into bed, tangled in a passionate embrace, recognition hit her.

"Is that Margery?" Ethan exclaimed. "With whom, though?" He squinted at the screen, trying to make out the mystery man.

Blue gasped as the pieces clicked. "That's Jack Malone! Remember, her neighbor that hated Tom?" This was an unexpected but revealing discovery.

Ethan let out a low whistle. "No wonder she was so quick to give up the evidence to Jameson. She was sleeping with the enemy!"

"This gives them both potential motive," Blue pointed out. "If Tom had this, it gave him power over Margery and Jack." Her mind whirred with the implications.

Ethan nodded slowly, eyes distant in thought. "Extramarital affairs can drive people to extreme measures when threatened with exposure." He turned to Blue, conviction shining in his eyes. "We need to take a very close look at these two."

Blue agreed, new possibilities swirling. The videos kept exposing more ethical breaches and secrets. But somewhere in the mess, the truth awaited. She could feel they were homing in on it.

Lost in thought, Blue and Ethan were caught off guard by the sound of Margery's heels clicking across the concrete floor. She appeared in the doorway, curiosity thinly veiled behind her polite expression.

"I hope you're finding everything in order," she began. "Did you need me to clarify anything before I see you out?"

Pausing the video, Blue turned to face Margery directly. "Actually, there is something we wanted to discuss." She gestured meaningfully at the screen.

Margery's gaze followed Blue's motion, landing on the frozen image of herself and Jack in a compromising embrace. For the briefest moment, her composure seemed to fracture. But she quickly schooled her features again.

"I suppose you have questions," she acknowledged, a muscle in her jaw feathering. "I assure you, my personal affairs are no one's business but my own." Defiance flashed in her eyes.

Ethan held up a placating hand. "We understand, and we apologize for the intrusion. But your...involvement with Jack could have bearing on the case."

Margery lifted her chin, shoulders squared. "Jack and I found solace together after years in unhappy marriages. I won't apologize for that." Her delivery was crisp and unapologetic.

Studying her closely, Blue saw no trace of shame or remorse. If anything, Margery seemed to relish their discomfort at her bold admission. It gave Blue pause. What else was this woman hiding?

Oblivious to their scrutiny, Margery checked her watch. "I'm afraid I'm late for my nail appointment. Do see yourselves out when you're finished here."

Blue's mind churned as she processed Margery's brazen admission. The affair gave both her and Jack ironclad motives if Tom had threatened to expose their

180

relationship. And there could be financial consequences for Margery as well.

"If Tom had evidence of your infidelity, it could impact your inheritance, correct?" she asked Margery point blank.

Margery's gaze sharpened, though her tone remained light. "Our prenuptial agreement was carefully constructed, as I'm sure you can imagine."

She examined her manicured nails before continuing. "But it's true my rights could be somewhat murkier if both parties were proven unfaithful."

Blue noted how she avoided directly answering the question, deflecting instead through implication. Everything about Margery's caginess in discussing the affair and its implications raised her suspicions higher.

Oblivious to Blue's scrutiny, Margery checked her watch again. "I really must be going. I've already missed my nail appointment." She moved briskly toward the garage door.

"One last thing," Ethan interjected before she could exit. "Did Tom ever confront you about the affair?" His gaze bored into her. "Threaten to expose it, perhaps?"

Margery paused, hand resting on the doorknob. For a fleeting moment, her eyes blazed with what looked like fury. But her face was serene again when she replied over her shoulder.

"Tom and I had an understanding, that's all you need to know."

Margery stood motionless by the garage door, hand frozen on the handle. Blue could see the tension in her posture, belying the composure of her expression. Clearly, there was more she was reticent to divulge.

Continuing her questioning, Blue asked pointedly, "If Tom had proof of your affair, do you really expect us to believe you wouldn't act to stop him exposing it?"

Margery whirled around, eyes blazing. "I've already told you - I did not kill my husband!" Her vehemence caught them both off guard.

Visibly regaining her equilibrium, Margery smoothed her skirt with a sharp motion. "If you're determined to pursue this line of questioning, you're wasting valuable time. I suggest you look to Sierra instead."

"Sierra?" Ethan echoed. "That would make sense, and she was already on my mental list."

Margery's lip curled in distaste. "The woman was utterly obsessed with him. She would have done anything to prevent losing her pampered lifestyle."

Before they could interject, she continued. "In fact, you'll find her residence is surveilled here as well. See for yourself what the brazen hussy was up to."

Exchanging a skeptical look with Ethan, Blue nevertheless navigated to the folder titled "Sierra Wells." Sure enough, there was live footage streaming from her home.

As they watched the empty living room, Margery made an impatient noise. "There, you see? No one home. Likely because she's realized the jig is up and fled town."

Chapter Eighteen

The video feed from Sierra's living room remained fixed, the empty interior betraying no clues. Growing impatient, Blue clicked ahead through older footage to see if anything illuminating had been captured.

Margery hovered nearby, watching over their shoulders. As the timestamp advanced to nighttime hours, the misty image of a couple entered the frame, caught in a heated embrace.

"How perfectly distasteful," Margery murmured, averting her gaze primly. "I'll leave you to review my husband's sordid affairs in private. I'd rather not witness such things."

She moved briskly toward the door but paused, turning back to add archly, "Do let me know if you uncover anything...notable." With that, she exited the garage, heels clicking across the driveway.

Now alone, Blue and Ethan exchanged an uneasy look. Both were reluctant to delve into recordings of Tom's intimate encounters, however pertinent they might be. The gross violation of privacy churned Blue's stomach.

Steeling herself, she scrolled ahead, watching the time stamp rather than the footage itself. If something directly tied to the murder was captured, they couldn't overlook it no matter how uncomfortable.

Finally, she stopped on a clip from two nights before Tom's death, based on the date. Taking a deep breath, she pressed play, hoping their unpleasant task was nearing an end.

The garage was claustrophobically silent as the surveillance footage continued rolling. Blue's palms were slick with nervous sweat, her stomach churning. Beside her, Ethan sat ramrod straight, jaw clenched tight. Both felt acute discomfort at witnessing such invasive recordings, but neither was willing to turn away.

The video advanced to nighttime hours on the fateful date of Tom's demise. Taking a deep, bracing breath, Blue clicked play, the misty footage flickering to life.

Unable to watch directly, she fixed her eyes on the corner of the screen. In her peripheral vision, she saw Sierra welcome Tom through her front door, body language relaxed and casual. As they settled onto the couch with glasses of wine, however, things shifted into more intimate territory.

Blue's face heated with embarrassment and she found herself studying the concrete floor. This felt like the lowest violation yet, peering into a private encounter never meant to be seen. Ethan shifted uncomfortably, clearing his throat.

"If, uh...if you want me to keep watching, so you don't have to..." he offered awkwardly.

Blue shook her head, wishing that was an option. "We both need to stay alert. Just in case." She knew the painful awkwardness was temporary.

As the minutes crawled by, Blue kept her gaze carefully averted. Out of her periphery, she detected Sierra and Tom moving into the bedroom, the living room emptying.

Unable to avoid noticing rapid movement and flashes of skin, Blue bit her lip hard, willing herself not to look directly. She offered up silent apologies, hoping Sierra would someday understand this intrusion had been necessary.

After interminable, tense minutes, the figures reappeared in the living room, now bitterly arguing based on their body language. Blue risked glancing up and saw them locked in a silent shouting match, faces twisted with rage.

Things reached a violent crescendo when Sierra seized a decorative lamp and swung it brutally at Tom's head. Blue gasped as it cracked against his temple, sending Tom crumpling motionless.

"My god," Ethan choked out hoarsely. They watched, horrified, as Sierra stood trembling over Tom's body, the lamp still gripped tightly in her fist. Chilling blankness overtook her expression before she dropped the lamp and began methodically wrapping Tom in trash bags.

Blue sat paralyzed as Sierra alone dragged Tom's shrouded form outside, returning minutes later with no outward signs of what had just occurred. The abrupt change was deeply unsettling.

Leaping into action, Blue grabbed her phone with shaking hands. As the call connected, Brock's familiar voice came over the line.

"Blue? Everything okay?"

"No, not at all," she responded shakily. "Brock, we found surveillance footage here showing the murder. Sierra killed Tom."

"What?! Are you absolutely certain?" Brock demanded.

"Yes, it's all on video. She hit him with a lamp and then dragged his body away. It's...it's awful." Her voice wavered, images flashing through her mind again.

Brock unleashed a string of shocked curses. When he spoke again, his tone was deadly serious. "Listen to me very carefully. Do not touch anything else. Leave the evidence intact. I'm on my way right now."

The rest of his instructions faded into the background as Blue's adrenaline crashed, leaving her limbs heavy and mind reeling. She distantly registered ending the call and relaying the news to Ethan. But Brock's stunned, horrified reaction echoed through her rattled thoughts.

Leaving the hidden surveillance room, Blue halted abruptly. Margery was no longer hovering nearby. The driveway sat empty, her car gone.

"She actually left," Blue said in surprise. Glancing around, she confirmed they were alone.

Beside her, Ethan frowned. "I guess she really did have somewhere to be."

A feeling of unease curled in Blue's stomach. Given the shocking truth about Sierra they'd just uncovered, Margery's abrupt departure felt unsettling.

"Maybe we should check the house, just in case," Ethan suggested.

They headed up the driveway and knocked sharply. No response came. Pressing their ears to the door, only silence could be heard within.

"I don't think she's here," Blue said. They exchanged a worried look.

Ethan's expression was grim. "You're thinking she went to confront Sierra herself, right?"

Blue chewed her lip anxiously and nodded. "We need to get over there. I'm worried about leaving her alone with Sierra right now." Desperation tinged her voice.

Nodding decisively, Ethan strode toward his motorcycle. "Let's go. We can't risk Margery being there unsupervised."

Chapter Nineteen

Pulling up outside the small bungalow, Blue took in the sight of Margery's Mercedes haphazardly parked at the curb. Climbing off of Ethan's motorcycle, anxiety swirled within her about what awaited inside the still house.

As they approached the front door marked by a cheerful wreath, the heavy silence weighed on Blue. She raised her fist and knocked sharply on the door. No response came. She and Ethan exchanged an uneasy look as she rapped her knuckles more insistently.

"Margery, it's Blue and Ethan!" she called out. "Open up if you're in there!"

Only ominous silence continued to answer her appeals. Blue chewed her lip anxiously, her mind conjuring distressing images of what could be transpiring within the quiet home.

Beside her, Ethan's forehead creased with concern. "Let's check around back," he suggested after a pause. "Maybe we can get a sense of what's happening before involving the police."

Nodding, Blue followed Ethan along the perimeter of the bungalow. Reaching the backyard, he slowly pushed open the tall wooden gate. Beyond lay a barren cement patio containing just some lawn furniture and a small grill. Blue's gaze instantly focused on the back door, standing slightly ajar several feet away.

Exchanging a tense look with Ethan, they cautiously moved onto the patio. As they approached the door, the only sounds were the chirping of birds in a nearby tree and the far-off drone of cars. Reaching the door, Ethan met Blue's eyes questioningly. At her small nod, he nudged it open wider. It swung inward without a sound, revealing the orderly kitchen within.

Blue's breath caught at the sight of cabinets standing wide open, surfaces cluttered with items strewn about haphazardly. It was clear signs of packing done in a hurry.

Before she could fully process the implications of the scene, hurried footsteps suddenly sounded from deeper within the house, growing louder. Panic flaring inside her, Blue grabbed Ethan's arm and pulled him down to crouch behind the kitchen island just as two figures appeared in the doorway.

Peering through the narrow gap afforded by their hiding spot, Blue instantly recognized Margery and Sierra entering the kitchen. Shock rippled through her at the sight, taking in their disheveled appearances and the suitcases they carried. Sierra set her bags on the table and began silently gathering items from throughout the house while Margery supervised.

Blue's mind reeled as she struggled to comprehend what she was witnessing. They were clearly packing Sierra's belongings, but why was Margery helping? Did she know the truth about Tom's murder? Sierra being the killer would explain their rushed efforts to flee town, but Margery's involvement perplexed and concerned Blue.

190

Beside her, Ethan watched intently with a deeply furrowed brow. Blue sensed he found the situation equally confusing and alarming. Neither had expected to find Margery actively assisting Sierra, despite their suspicions that she had come here alone. They needed answers, but first had to slip away unseen themselves.

Remaining hidden behind the island, Blue observed mutely as Margery and Sierra continued moving through the house, gathering Sierra's possessions to add to the suitcases. Both women's body language was tense and urgent as they worked. Soon the two large suitcases atop the kitchen table were overflowing with clothing and personal items.

With the bags stuffed to capacity and zipped closed, Margery did a quick survey of the room. "I think that's everything," she pronounced briskly. "We need to move quickly now."

Picking up one of the heavy suitcases, she headed toward the living room and front door, Sierra close behind with the other. As their footsteps rapidly faded down the hall, Blue turned to Ethan with anxiety and confusion swirling through her. His solemn expression reflected her own lack of comprehension about the scene they had just secretly witnessed.

"Why is Margery helping her flee town?" Blue whispered urgently once the women's footsteps had receded. "She has to know Sierra killed Tom, right?"

Ethan just shook his head, clearly as much at a loss to explain Margery's actions and involvement as Blue was.

"I'm not sure what's going on between them," he admitted grimly after a pause. "But we need to get some answers fast, before Sierra disappears."

Nodding anxiously, Blue knew he was right. The sound of a car door closing echoed from the front of the house - they were already loading up the Mercedes. Time was running out to catch them and uncover the truth.

With no other choice, Blue and Ethan quickly slipped out the back door and crept alongside the house before Margery and Sierra could drive away. Peering around the corner, they saw the two women busily packing the trunk, focused solely on their urgent task. Blue knew time was running out to get the answers they desperately needed.

Exchanging a tense nod with Ethan, they briskly rounded the corner and approached the two women just as they were closing the trunk, packed full of Sierra's bags.

"Margery!" Blue called out sharply, causing both women to freeze in place. "What's going on here?"

Margery's eyes blew wide with shock, her gaze landing on Blue and Ethan. Sierra instantly paled, dropping her eyes to the ground. A suspended moment followed as they all stood motionless.

Then Margery straightened, smoothing her features into a carefully composed mask. "Well, you both certainly have a penchant for turning up unexpectedly," she said coolly.

She eyed them both with thinly veiled irritation. "I suppose you want some sort of explanation."

Blue crossed her arms challengingly. "That would be an excellent start." Beside her, Ethan stood silent and imposing, letting his sturdy presence underscore her demand.

Margery let out an exaggerated sigh, as if greatly inconvenienced. "Oh, very well then. But let's take this inside, shall we? No need to have a scene out on the street." Her tone was patently false.

Exchanging a skeptical look with Ethan, Blue reluctantly followed Margery and Sierra back into the house, now emptied of Sierra's belongings. The sterile interior felt eerily quiet and still.

Once seated stiffly in the living room, Margery arranged herself with forced elegance, folding her hands neatly in her lap. Sierra perched tensely on the couch edge, staring fixedly at the floor.

"I suppose you're wondering why I'm helping Sierra hastily leave town," Margery began, still feigning casual annoyance.

"The thought had crossed my mind, yes," Blue replied dryly.

Margery's eyes narrowed fractionally before she seemed to decide on a course of action. Dropping all pretenses, she lifted her chin and met Blue's gaze directly.

"The truth is, I hired Sierra several months ago as part of a calculated plan," she stated bluntly. "I wanted her to seduce Tom and gather evidence of his chronic adultery."

Stunned silence met this matter-of-fact admission. Blue's mind reeled as she tried to absorb this unexpected revelation. Beside her, Ethan appeared equally blindsided.

"You...hired her for that purpose?" he finally managed to say, shock evident in his tone.

"I did," Margery confirmed crisply, her face impassive. "I had grown aware of Tom's...wandering eye. Sierra was meant to lure him into a compromising situation, providing grounds for divorce."

Blue stared wordlessly at the composed blonde, seeing Margery in a startling new light. This astonishing confession suddenly made her behavior comprehensible - the lack of grief, the urgency to help Sierra escape.

"So you knew who she was all along," Blue said slowly, still processing the information. "You weren't just helping a stranger. You were protecting someone in your employ."

Margery's lips twisted sardonically. "Essentially, yes. Though I didn't realize Sierra's involvement would escalate to...this." Her façade cracked briefly with discomfort before smoothing over.

"But I cannot have her implicating me now," she continued briskly. "My only concern is removing any connection."

Blue knew they were running out of time to uncover the full truth.

Taking a subtle breath, she met Margery's gaze. "You admitted that you assumed Sierra killed Tom in self-defense, correct?"

Margery nodded. "Yes, that was my belief at the time."

"But you didn't actually see the garage footage showing the murder?" Blue pressed.

"No, I left before you reviewed those recordings," Margery confirmed, confusion entering her eyes.

Blue hesitated briefly before replying. "Because what the video revealed was Sierra attacking Tom completely unprovoked in a fit of rage."

Margery went utterly still, staring at Blue. "What? No, that can't be..." she whispered in disbelief.

"It's true," Ethan confirmed grimly. "The footage clearly shows Sierra striking Tom without physical provocation. His murder was an act of fury, not self-defense."

As his blunt words sank in, Margery recoiled as if struck, horror dawning on her face. "No, no, I was so certain..." she choked out unsteadily.

Whirling to face Sierra, indignation broke through her anguish. "You told me he attacked you first! That you had no choice but to defend yourself! Was that all lies?"

Sierra shrank under Margery's burning stare. After long moments, she finally lifted her head, eyes full of turmoil. "It's true, I killed him," she admitted hoarsely...

Blue hesitated to break the tense silence. Sierra had just confessed to murdering Tom in a fit of rage, shattering Margery's perception of events.

Both women now sat raw and exposed, struggling to process Sierra's deceit. Blue exchanged an uneasy look with Ethan, unsure if they should interrupt this emotionally fraught moment. But the clock was ticking - they still needed the full truth from Sierra.

Clearing her throat gently, Blue met the murderer's downcast eyes. "I know this is deeply painful," she began softly. "But we need you to explain exactly what happened that night...and why."

Sierra flinched at her words, arms wrapped tightly around herself. A long moment passed before she lifted her head, eyes brimming with emotion.

"You're right, you deserve the full truth," she whispered hoarsely. Taking a shuddering breath, Sierra continued, her voice ragged.

"That night, I asked Tom to finally leave Margery for me. I told him..." She faltered briefly. "I lied and told him I was pregnant. I thought it would make him stay."

Margery inhaled sharply but remained silent. Nodding for her to continue, Blue kept her expression carefully neutral.

"But he just got angry," Sierra said miserably. "He wrote me a check for an abortion and said we were done for good. He was so cold, so dismissive..."

Her breath hitched on what sounded like a sob. "I realized then that he never cared about me. That our whole relationship was a lie. Something inside me just...snapped."

They could see Sierra retreating into her memories, reliving the rage she had felt. "I saw red. All I could think was how he'd ruined my life and used me. I hated him in that moment."

Her voice dropped to a ragged whisper. "Before I even knew what I was doing, I had grabbed the lamp and was striking him. I was blinded by this fiery fury, fueled by a twisted desire for revenge."

Sierra's eyes took on a distant sheen. "Afterwards, seeing him lying there lifeless...the haze of anger lifted. Suddenly I was terrified. I panicked and tried to hide what I'd done."

As her confession ended, Sierra's shoulders slumped in defeat. The room rang with stunned silence, the ugliness of her actions laid bare between them.

Margery seemed frozen, gazing at Sierra as if seeing a stranger sitting there. "So it truly was a crime of passion," she said faintly. "Not self-defense at all."

Sierra just nodded wretchedly under her disillusioned stare. Everything between them had curdled into deceit in one shattering instant.

Letting out a slow breath, Blue tried to process the dark intensity of emotions that could drive someone to commit such a heinous crime. Beside her, Ethan wore a similarly grave expression.

Glancing his way, Blue knew they were of one mind - the time had come to transfer Sierra into police custody, before anything more went awry. There would be ample time later to further untangle motives and meanings.

First, they needed to ensure Sierra faced justice for her actions. Meeting Ethan's eyes, Blue tipped her head meaningfully toward the hallway in a silent request. Understanding her intent, Ethan shifted subtly to block the exit.

Turning back to Sierra's hunched form, Blue adopted a gentle but firm tone. "Thank you for being honest with us," she began diplomatically. "I know that was difficult. But now, for everyone's safety, we need to notify the authorities."

As expected, panic flared in Sierra's eyes at this. But to Blue's surprise, her shoulders slumped again in defeat a moment later. It seemed the fight had gone out of her.

"Just please, allow me a moment to clean myself up first," Sierra requested dully. "I'd like to retain a shred of dignity when they take me away."

Blue hesitated, wavering between sympathy and wariness. Before she could respond, Ethan stepped in diplomatically.

"Of course," he soothed. "We'll accompany you, and just be a quick moment." Sierra nodded bleakly and rose to her feet.

As she moved toward the bathroom, Blue and Ethan flanked her closely. The risk of her slipping away remained high.

Margery didn't even lift her gaze as they shuffled past, still reeling from the ugly truth laid bare.

Crowding into the small bathroom, Blue kept a close eye on Sierra as she splashed water on her face and neatened her disheveled hair with trembling hands. Ethan stood vigilant in the doorway.

"Thank you for at least allowing me this shred of dignity," Sierra said quietly as she straightened.

Blue nodded, feeling a flicker of sympathy for the broken woman. But she hardened her resolve, reminding herself of the heinous crime Sierra had committed.

With the solemn prisoner arrayed as respectably as possible under the circumstances, they ventured back down the hall toward Margery's unnervingly still form.

But they had only gone a few steps when Sierra suddenly gasped and recoiled, staring past Blue in horror. Whipping around, Blue's heart jolted at the sight of a large, ominous brown recluse spider crawling along the wall just inches from where they stood.

"Get it away!" Sierra shrieked, panic shrill in her voice. Blind terror consumed her features as she scrabbled frantically at Blue's arm.

Caught off guard by her extreme reaction, Blue tried vainly to calm the hysterical woman now clawing desperately at her in an attempt to flee the approaching spider.

"It's okay, just stay still!" Blue urged, even as Sierra continued thrashing wildly against her. But irrational fear had hijacked any reasoning.

Ethan hurried back to try and restrain Sierra's flailing limbs. But she fought viciously, nails raking his forearms. Grunting in pain, Ethan struggled to control her convulsing form.

"Calm down, it's just a spider!" he gritted out through the chaos. But Sierra was beyond hearing, consumed by blind animal panic.

Intent on helping Ethan restrain her, Blue made the mistake of shifting her hold. With an opening suddenly created, Sierra broke free and made a frantic bolt for the front door.

"Stop!" Blue yelled, giving chase. Ethan pounded after them down the hall. They converged on Sierra just as her shaking hands wrenched the door open.

Acting on instinct, Blue tackled her around the waist. They crashed painfully to the floor in a tangle of limbs. Sierra fought like a wild animal, screaming and clawing.

Pinning her flailing arms took all Blue's strength. Ethan grabbed her kicking feet, trying to avoid her vicious heels. Sierra's voice dissolved into incoherent shrieking.

Abruptly, heavy footsteps pounded up the porch steps. Brock's formidable frame filled the doorway, taking in the violent chaos. His gaze landed on Sierra's contorted, crimson face.

"Need some help here!" Ethan grit out, still struggling to subdue her manic thrashing. Brock immediately moved to assist, using his substantial bulk to pin her bucking torso.

Between the three of them, they finally managed to restrain her enough for Brock to cuff her hands. Sierra tugged uselessly against the metal restraints, screaming hoarse obscenities.

Releasing his hold slowly, Brock eyed the hysterical woman with profound confusion. "What in blazes is going on here?" he demanded, scowling between Blue and Ethan still sprawled on the floor.

"She totally lost it when she saw a spider," Blue explained breathlessly, getting unsteadily to her feet. "Just went into sheer panic mode trying to escape."

Brock absorbed this with a shake of his head. Sierra had collapsed into heaving sobs on the floor beside him. The fight seemed to have fully drained from her body.

"Please, I'm sorry," she wept almost incoherently. "I didn't mean to...the spider...please..." Her pleas dissolved into inarticulate whimpering.

Kneeling down beside her, Brock spoke with calm authority. "Get yourself together now. No more of this outburst business, do you understand?"

At his stern tone, Sierra visibly tried to compose herself, reduced to hiccupping whimpers. Margery still sat numbly nearby, observing it all with red-rimmed eyes.

Hauling Sierra to her feet, Brock addressed them wearily. "I don't even want to know what other chaos you've caused today. But it's clear now that she needs to be in police custody."

Sierra stood docilely, energy depleted, as Brock Mirandized her and led her haltingly outside. As the patrol car pulled away, its lights flashing mutely, Blue released a breath she hadn't realized she was holding.

It was over at last. Margery remained behind, looking small and broken amidst the wreckage. In their own ways, both women would now pay a steep price.

Exchanging exhausted looks with Ethan, Blue wanted nothing more than to collapse into bed and sleep for a week. But there was still Margery to deal with.

Approaching her gingerly, Blue asked, "Will you be all right getting home?"

Margery just gazed at her with empty eyes. "I'll manage, thank you," she murmured distantly.

Watching stoically as the patrol car carrying Sierra pulled away, its lights flashing mutely, Blue released a breath she'd been holding. It was over now, for better or worse.

The faint sound of boots on pavement made Blue turn to see Brock striding back up the walkway, his expression thunderous. She braced herself for the reprimand sure to come.

Stopping before them, Brock crossed his arms and surveyed Blue and Ethan severely. "Would either of you care to explain what in blazes you were thinking?" he bit out.

Blue winced, dropping her eyes. She had no good excuse for their actions.

When she didn't immediately respond, Brock continued berating them sharply. "You should have stayed out of this investigation and let me handle things. Instead, you went behind my back."

His scowl deepened. "Do you have any idea the position you've put me in as the investigating officer? The two of you have thoroughly compromised this crime scene and inserted yourself directly into the middle of a homicide case!"

Chastened, Blue scuffed her shoe against the pavement. She couldn't refute Brock's words. Beside her, Ethan stood straight-backed but silent under the reprimand.

Releasing an irritated breath, Brock pressed on. "I hope you can comprehend the severity of the situation now and why we have proper protocols for pursuing leads and gathering evidence."

Finally lifting her head, Blue hastened to reply. "We understand completely, and we're so sorry for interfering. It was a terrible lapse in judgment." She nudged Ethan subtly.

"Absolutely," he readily agreed. "It won't happen again. We shouldn't have overstepped our role."

Rubbing a hand over his jaw, Brock studied them critically for a long moment. When he spoke again, his tone had lost some of its hard edge.

"Look, I know you both meant well and were only trying to uncover the truth. But taking matters into your own hands could have had dire consequences. Proper procedure must be followed to avoid disaster."

Margery still sat morosely on the porch nearby, seemingly lost inside her own grim thoughts.

Following Brock's gaze, Blue felt a pang of sympathy for the broken woman. "We didn't intend for any of this to happen," she offered sincerely. "It just seemed crucial to find answers quickly before Sierra could flee. But we acted rashly, and we're deeply sorry for that."

Brock sighed heavily but gave a gruff nod. "What's done is done. We'll just have to handle this mess from here." Glancing between them sternly again, he added, "But if either of you interfere in my cases again, there will be severe repercussions. Are we crystal clear?"

"Yes, sir," Blue and Ethan answered in unison, properly chastised.

"Good. Then my advice is to go home and reflect on how your actions could have seriously jeopardized bringing a murderer to justice." His tone was severe but not unkind.

Turning toward his car, Brock added brusquely, "I'll handle things from here. Despite the chaotic nature of its acquisition, the evidence against Sierra is overwhelming.

She'll remain in police custody while I build an airtight case against her."

Climbing wearily into his cruiser, Brock gave them one last quelling look. "I'll be in touch soon to get your full statements. Until then, stay out of trouble and let me do my job."

With that, he started the engine and pulled smoothly away down the street, leaving them standing abashedly in his wake. Exchanging embarrassed looks, they both recognized the truth in Brock's harsh lecture.

"I guess we really made a mess of things," Blue admitted quietly.

Ethan blew out a rueful breath. "Well, Deputy Do-Right sure ripped us a new one. But I guess we should've let him handle it."

Scuffing her shoe, Blue nodded regretfully. "All's well that ends well, at least Sierra's in custody."

"True," Ethan agreed. "Though clearly we're the superior investigators." He glanced at Margery's hunched form on the porch steps. "Anyway, time we clear out and let everyone move on from this mess."

Following his gaze, Blue felt sympathy for the disillusioned woman. Their lives would be irrevocably changed by these traumatic events. But the darkness shrouding Tom's murder had finally been exposed. Time to close this grim chapter.

Bidding Margery a subdued farewell, Blue wearily climbed onto Ethan's motorcycle. As they pulled away, Margery's small, solitary form receded in the side mirror.

Chapter Twenty

The drive back to Blue's house passed in weary silence. Blue rested her aching head against the window, watching the familiar streets roll by without really seeing them. Her mind felt overloaded trying to process the day's dark events.

Beside her, Ethan kept his gaze fixed steadily on the road ahead. He seemed content to let her ruminate quietly. Blue felt grateful for his intuitive understanding.

Turning onto her tree-lined street, Ethan pulled up outside Blue's charming white two-story house. Killing the engine, he turned to her with concern.

"Will you be all right getting inside on your own?" he asked gently. "Or should I walk you in?"

Blue managed a tired smile. "I'll be fine, don't worry. Thank you for the ride though. And for everything today. Actually, would you like to come in for a little while? I'm sure Pepper will want to hear what happened too."

Looking mildly surprised but pleased, Ethan readily agreed.

Climbing stiffly from the motorcycle, Blue led the way up the front path and unlocked her sky-blue door. Stepping inside, she flicked on the lights and called out for her sister and cat.

Rapid footsteps sounded, and Pepper came hurrying around the corner. Surprise registered on her face at seeing Ethan hovering behind Blue.

"Oh, hi, Ethan! Wasn't expecting to see you here," she recovered smoothly. Tiffany slunk around the corner next, eyeing Ethan suspiciously before trotting away.

"Let's sit, we have quite the day to recap," Blue said, leading them into the cozy living room. She recounted the dramatic events at Sierra's house, with Ethan adding details.

Finishing her account of Sierra's arrest, Blue said, "So it was certainly a rollercoaster. But the truth is out now."

"That's insane, I can't believe you tackled a murderer!" Pepper exclaimed in awe.

Blue chuckled tiredly. "Hopefully, no more tackling killers for me. I think I'm done with amateur sleuthing."

Beside her, Ethan made a noise of amusement.

Taking initiative, Blue then stretched and stood. "Well, I'm famished. How about I whip up some dinner for us all?"

After suggesting dinner, Blue linked arms with Pepper and headed to the kitchen. "Let's whip up some comfort food - how about your famous mac and cheese?"

"Ooh, yes! That sounds perfect," Pepper agreed readily. As she gathered ingredients, Blue retrieved vegetables from the fridge for a salad.

Noticing Ethan lingering uncertainly by the entry, Blue gave him a warm smile. "You're welcome to stay for dinner too if you'd like, Ethan."

Looking surprised but pleased by the invitation, Ethan said, "If you're sure I wouldn't be imposing, I'd love to." He took a seat at the worn wooden kitchen table.

Soon the kitchen was filled with the nostalgic sounds and scents of cooking. Pepper busied herself at the stove, humming as she made the cheesy pasta. "This mac and cheese recipe was Grandma's specialty," she told Ethan. "It's super creamy and comforting."

"It smells amazing already," Ethan said sincerely. "What can I do to help?"

"You just relax, you're our guest!" Blue assured him as she chopped vegetables for the salad.

As she worked, Blue's mind turned to the fledgling ideas she'd been gathering for a new line of artisanal chocolates. The creative energy in the room fueled her enthusiasm.

"You know, I've been thinking of trying some new chocolate recipes for the shop," she mused aloud. "Really focusing on quality ingredients and unique flavor combos."

"Oooh, we should infuse them with herbs and edible flowers!" Pepper suggested eagerly, glancing up from the simmering pasta pot. "Lavender or rosemary would be so nice."

Growing more animated as she brainstormed, Blue gesticulated with the salad tongs as she spoke. "Yes, that's such a great idea! We could do chocolates with a subtle floral taste. Really elegant and unconventional."

"Ooh, I love that!" Pepper grinned. "We should look up recipes for herbal infusion. And we could do some with spices too, like cinnamon or cardamom."

Nodding enthusiastically, Blue became fully engrossed describing her visions for the new confections, with Pepper eagerly contributing ideas.

"I'm picturing gem-shaped ones in rose gold or midnight blue foil. And some with a rustic look, like dusted with edible glitter or gold leaf," Blue said dreamily.

The sisters enthusiastically discussed different cacao percentages, flavor pairings, possible shapes and packaging. Ethan listened with interest, asking the occasional question.

After serving the food and settling at the table, the lively chocolate brainstorming continued. "We'll have to do lots of taste testing to get the flavors just right," Pepper said.

"And we'll only source the highest quality chocolate for these confections," Blue added. "I can't wait to get creative and start formulating recipes!"

Their passion was irrepressible as they bantered back and forth about ingredients, textures, and designing the perfect elegantly styled boxes for the chocolates. The new line felt brimming with potential.

Smiling across the table at Ethan, Blue told him warmly, "We can't wait for you to be the first to try our new creations once they're ready!"

"I'm honored," Ethan replied, eyes crinkling charmingly at the corners. "And a little nervous - I'll have very high expectations now!" His gentle teasing made Blue's cheeks grow warm.

As the lively dinner conversation came to a natural lull, Pepper leaned back in her chair with a satisfied smile. "That was delicious. Your mac and cheese is the best comfort food ever," she told Blue appreciatively.

Blue smiled, touched by the praise. "Well, I can't take credit - Grandma's recipe is the real star here."

Beside her, Ethan made a noise of agreement as he finished his last bite. "It really was incredible. My compliments to both the chefs."

Across the table, Pepper stifled a small yawn behind one hand. "Well, I'm completely stuffed and ready for an early night." She stood and gathered her plate to rinse in the sink.

"I think I'll head up and crash," she said, moving toward the hallway. Pausing, she added casually, "Tiffany is welcome to join me if she's tired too."

The cat stretched languidly before gracefully hopping down to follow Pepper upstairs. Blue suppressed a smile at her sister's transparent attempt to give her privacy with Ethan.

"Sleep well, you two," she called after them fondly. Their footsteps receded down the hall until only she and Ethan remained in the cozy kitchen.

Turning back to him, Blue asked, "Would you like any coffee or tea? Or perhaps something sweet from the shop?"

Ethan smiled and shook his head. "Thank you, but I'm quite satisfied. That was a perfect meal." He leaned back comfortably in his chair, at ease in the sanctuary of her home.

"I'm glad you stayed," Blue told him sincerely. "After the intensity of today, having your company means a lot." She hoped the words conveyed her depth of feeling.

Ethan's dark eyes softened. "Of course. I'm thankful anytime I get to spend with you." His gentle candor never failed to make Blue's heart flutter.

They chatted comfortably about lighter topics for a while - funny customer stories, their favorite books, predictions for the upcoming town festival. Blue found herself leaning closer, chin propped on one hand, as she soaked up their cozy conversation.

A natural lull eventually descended. In the pause, Ethan straightened slightly in his chair, seeming to gather his nerve. "Blue, there's something I've been wanting to ask you."

Her pulse quickened at his change in tone, though she kept her expression neutral. "Oh? What's that?"

Rubbing the back of his neck almost shyly, Ethan met her gaze. "I was hoping...that is, if you're interested...you might like to go out to dinner with me sometime?" His eyes were tentatively hopeful behind his glasses. "On an actual date, I mean."

Warm pleasure blossomed in Blue's chest. Unable to contain her smile, she replied, "I would love that. Truly." It felt good to finally voice the attraction simmering between them out loud.

Ethan's face broke into an endearingly crooked grin, relief and delight evident. "Yeah? I'm really glad to hear that." He seemed momentarily at a loss for words, which Blue found incredibly charming.

Her heart was still fluttering wildly, hardly believing this wonderful man had just asked her on a real date. She couldn't wait to see where this new path would lead.

Glancing at the clock, Ethan gave her a regretful look. "I should probably get going and let you rest. But perhaps I could call you tomorrow and we could choose a day for dinner? If that sounds all right?"

"I'd like that a lot," Blue assured him warmly. She walked him to the front door, hyperaware of his nearness in the entryway. Pausing, Ethan met her gaze.

"Thank you again for tonight. For...everything." The depth of emotion in his voice made her shiver.

Then he leaned in and placed a feather-light kiss on her cheek that left her skin tingling. With a final adoring look, he slipped out into the night, leaving Blue's heart brimming with happiness.

Chapter Twenty-One

After watching Ethan's taillights disappear down the street, a wide smile still lingered on Blue's face. Closing the front door, she pressed her hands to warm cheeks, hardly able to contain her giddiness.

Still floating on cloud nine, Blue wandered back to the cozy kitchen. She considered making some soothing chamomile tea, wanting to unwind before bed.

A nice cup of tea sounded perfect right now. As she rummaged in the cupboard for a mug, her eyes landed on an unopened bottle of red wine sitting on the counter.

Blue paused in surprise. She didn't remember buying any wine recently. Shrugging, she figured she must have picked it up a while ago and she forgot about it. A celebratory glass sounded even better than tea.

Retrieving a wine glass from the cabinet, Blue poured herself a generous helping. She inhaled the rich oak notes appreciatively before taking a leisurely sip, letting the complex flavor roll over her tongue. Perfect.

Glass in hand, she wandered back to the living room and curled up contentedly on the sofa. The remote sat invitingly on the coffee table. Scrolling through options, Blue settled on a new romantic comedy to enjoy.

As the movie's opening credits began rolling, she took another smooth sip of wine, sinking back into the soft couch cushions. The story followed a busy career woman too focused on work to find love, until she met a charming carpenter hired to renovate her kitchen. Predictable, but cute.

About twenty minutes into the film, as the leads were enjoying their inevitable meet-cute scene, a sharp knock sounded from the front of the house. Blue jumped, wine sloshing dangerously close to the rim of her glass. Who could that be at this hour?

Muting the TV, Blue set her wine down and hurried to the foyer, curiosity rising. She wasn't expecting anyone else tonight. Had Ethan forgotten something? A foolish part of her hoped he'd returned simply because he missed her already, but she pushed that farfetched thought away.

Smoothing her hair and straightening her rumpled blouse, Blue took a breath before turning the knob and pulling the door open. Surprise flashed through her at the sight of Brock filling the entryway, still in his uniform.

"Brock! Hello again," Blue stammered, confusion swirling. "Is everything okay?" Her thoughts flew to Sierra in police custody. Had something gone wrong?

Brock removed his hat, fiddling with the brim. "Evening, Blue. Sorry to drop by unannounced so late, but there's something I was hoping to discuss with you." He shifted his weight, seeming uncharacteristically ill at ease. "May I come in for a moment?"

"Of course!" Blue recovered her manners, stepping back hurriedly. "Please, make yourself comfortable." She led the way to the living room, internally debating whether to offer him the wine. Best not, given he was still on duty.

Settling somewhat stiffly on the couch, Brock ran a hand over his short hair and cleared his throat. "I apologize for intruding on your evening like this. I just wanted to speak with you privately, away from the station."

Perching across from him, Blue gave what she hoped was an encouraging look. "It's no intrusion at all. I'm happy to talk about anything on your mind." Despite her reassuring tone, curiosity was eating her alive. Why was he being so formal?

Brock nodded, seeming to gather his resolve. Finally meeting her gaze directly, he spoke. "The truth is, I came here tonight because...because I find myself thinking about you more and more, Blue. In a personal way." His admission hovered in the air between them.

Blue's mind went blank, stunned into silence. Whatever she had expected, a declaration of romantic interest from Brock was not it. They had been friends for so long, and he has never shown any interest. Not as far as she'd noticed, anyway... She opened her mouth but no words emerged.

Clearing his throat again, Brock pressed on in a rush. "I know we've been friends for years, but lately I've started feeling drawn to you as more than that, Blue. I'd like the chance to explore those feelings between us if you're willing. Would you go to dinner with me this weekend?" His stern features were uncharacteristically soft and vulnerable.

Heart thudding wildly, Blue desperately tried to gather her whirling thoughts. Mere hours ago, she had happily agreed to a date with Ethan, who she was quickly coming to care for deeply.

Yet here was kind, solid Brock, one of her oldest and dearest friends, asking for that same chance. She had no idea how to gracefully navigate this unprecedented situation.

Seeing Brock's expectant expression growing worried at her prolonged silence, Blue floundered to respond. "I'm so flattered, truly," she began haltingly. "It means the world that you would ask. I just..."

How could she let him down gently, without damaging their longtime friendship? Her reluctance must have shown on her face. Brock's shoulders slumped slightly.

"There's someone else, isn't there?" His voice was resigned but free of bitterness. He even gave her a small, bittersweet smile. "I should've known he would have already asked."

Unsure what to say, Blue could only offer a helpless, apologetic look. But Brock waved it off kindly. "Please, no need to explain. I understand, and I hope we can still be friends."

"Of course!" Blue assured him fervently, incredibly grateful for his gracious reaction. But uncertainty still gnawed at her as Brock stood to leave. She walked him to the door, hoping the awkwardness between them would quickly fade.

Pausing on the threshold, Brock squeezed her hand lightly. "Thank you for always being open with me. I truly meant what I said - you're an incredible woman, Blue. Don't forget." With that, he descended the steps into the pooling shadows, leaving Blue's emotions churning.

But as she watched him get into his cruiser and pull away, a thought niggled at the back of her mind. That thought was, *If he'd given me time to answer, I think I might have said yes.*

Blue was caught off guard by this revelation. Had she been waiting all these years for Brock to ask?

And if so, now what?

"A thought for tomorrow," she said to the empty entryway as she yawned and stretched.

Blue rested her forehead against the smooth wood for a moment as she tried to process the unexpected turn of events. She cared deeply for Brock as her longtime friend. But pursuing anything romantic felt…

Pushing off the door with a sigh, Blue began wearily climbing the stairs to her bedroom. The emotional ups and downs of the day had left her drained. Maybe tomorrow things would seem clearer.

She had only reached the landing when her cell phone suddenly rang shrilly from her pocket. Jolting in surprise, Blue fished it out hastily. Her pulse stuttered slightly because she thought she saw Brock's name flash across the screen.

Of course he was calling - they really needed to discuss things openly and repair any hurt feelings between them. Taking a fortifying breath, Blue answered the call.

"Hi, Brock, I'm so glad you called..." she began earnestly but was cut off by a brusque female voice.

"Well, it's about time you picked up!" Aunt Libby interrupted impatiently. "Honestly, young people and their addiction to screens these days. It's like I'm talking to myself whenever I call."

Blue bit back a sharp retort, irritation flaring. Trust her opinionated aunt to insert herself at precisely the wrong moment.

"My apologies, Aunt Libby. It's been a bit of an evening," Blue responded as politely as she could muster. "Was there something specific you needed?"

"As a matter of fact, there is," her aunt declared importantly. "I know you've been struggling to build your little candy hobby into something profitable, so I've taken it upon myself to secure you a meeting with the dean of the local college."

Blue's irritation spiked higher. "My candy shop is not just a hobby, it's a successful small business," she couldn't help correcting testily.

Libby barreled on undeterred. "Yes, well, a nice little shop is all well and good, dear, but you're nearly thirty now. It's time to consider a real career and getting serious about your future."

Clenching her free hand, Blue forced herself to take a calming breath. Her traditionalist aunt had never supported her dream of running her own candy shop, believing Blue should have a more "respectable" career. Their values clashed irreconcilably at times.

"With all due respect, I'm very serious about my business," Blue said evenly. "I happen to find it incredibly fulfilling, and I'm proud of what I've built."

Her aunt tutted disapprovingly. "It's a pleasant little venture I'm sure, but it's hardly a stable long-term option for someone your age."

Before Blue could respond angrily, Libby continued. "Luckily, I know people on the college board, and was able to convince the dean to meet with you. With some retraining, I'm sure we can get you on a proper career path."

Losing the battle to rein in her temper, Blue retorted, "I appreciate you thinking of me, but I neither want nor need you interfering with my career like this. I'm very happy running my own business, which is doing better than ever. And I am not almost thirty."

"Oh, don't be silly," Libby scoffed. "You may find puttering around that shop enjoyable for now, but a steady paycheck and benefits are what you need. Don't throw away this opportunity."

Anger simmered hotly in Blue's chest. "I built this shop through years of hard work and personal sacrifice. And we're thriving - sales have never been better!"

"That's wonderful for now, but no reason to limit your options," Libby replied breezily. "A job in accounting or management would provide much more stability. You don't want to waste your potential."

Clenching her jaw, Blue fought to control her mounting frustration. Her aunt refused to actually hear anything she said.

"I'm not interested in totally changing careers," she bit out sharply. "I love running my shop, and I'm proud of what I've accomplished. This isn't just temporary for me - it's my dream, and I've made it succeed."

Libby sighed heavily. "Dreams are all well and good, dear. But at some point, you have to get realistic. You're not getting any younger, and it's time to think seriously about committing to a real profession."

"Enough!" Blue finally shouted, patience snapping. "I don't need you constantly second-guessing my choices and pressuring me to be someone I'm not. This shop makes me happier than any office job ever could. Why can't you just support me?"

"Lower your voice, there's no need for hysterics," her aunt said sternly. "I'm trying to prevent you from wasting your potential. Someday you'll thank me for this."

Clenching her eyes shut, Blue inhaled slowly through her nose, trying desperately to calm down before she said something unforgivable. This conversation was going nowhere productive.

"I have to go now," she finally grit out. "Thank you again for thinking of me. Goodbye."

Before Libby could launch into a new barrage, Blue quickly ended the call and dropped her phone on the bed, covering her face with her hands. Arguing with her aunt was utterly draining. She focused on taking deep, centering breaths, willing her irritation to fade.

Rubbing her temples wearily, Blue tried redirecting her thoughts to Ethan and their promising new relationship. She wouldn't let her aunt's arrogance and criticism distract her from what mattered.

Picking up her phone, she typed out a quick goodnight text to Ethan about the lovely evening they'd shared. There - focusing on the positives. With him in her thoughts, her aunt's misguided views no longer held power to upset her.

She took a few more deep breaths to calm herself before deciding to check on Pepper and say goodnight. Hopefully, her cheery sister would help get her mind off the argument.

Leaving her room, Blue headed down the hall to Pepper's bedroom and knocked softly. "Pep? You still awake?" No response came. She knocked once more, then slowly turned the knob and peeked inside.

The room was empty, the bed neatly made. Blue's brow furrowed. Where had Pepper gone? She must have slipped out while Blue was dealing with their aunt's call.

"Pepper?" Blue called loudly as she quickly checked the other upstairs rooms just in case. No reply. Growing worried now, she hurried down to the main floor, scanning the quiet living room and dark kitchen. The house was still.

Blue hurried downstairs looking for Pepper, starting to really worry. She was just about to call Brock when in sauntered Tiffany, her black fur sleek and shiny.

"Hey, girl, what's the sitch?" the cat greeted her casually in a Valley girl accent. "Looking for your little sis again?"

Blue blinked in surprise at Tiffany's manner of speaking but quickly recovered. "Yes, do you know where Pepper went?"

Examining her paws lazily, Tiffany replied, "Oh, yeah, your sister, like, totally snuck out again. She's been doing that a lot lately, y'know?"

Blue gaped at her familiar. "What do you mean she's been sneaking out? Why didn't you tell me?" Hurt mixed with her shock that Tiffany had kept this secret.

The cat lifted one furry shoulder. "I just figured you already knew and were cool with it, so I didn't wanna harsh your mellow, ya feel? Anyway, girl, when are you gonna finally take me to the mall? I wanna visit my gal Brenda at the pet store!"

Frustration flared in Blue at that flippant response. "Don't try to change the subject!" she admonished. "You should've told me Pepper was sneaking out!"

Tiffany merely blinked her wide eyes. "Chill out, girl. Like I said, I thought you were handling it." She stood and stretched leisurely. "Anywho, hit me up when you wanna take me to the mall, 'kay?" Tossing Blue a departing wink, she sauntered casually from the room.

Blue pressed a hand to her now aching temples. Her familiar's attitude could be so frustrating! But she had bigger things to worry about.

Epilogue

Sitting tensely on the edge of Pepper's bed, Blue anxiously awaited her sister's return. The teen had been sneaking out at night unbeknownst to her, and Blue intended to get answers.

Just as the first pale light of dawn crept over the horizon, a faint scuffing sound came from the window. Whipping around, Blue saw Pepper attempting to quietly climb back inside.

"Where have you been all night?" Blue demanded, ready to lay into her sister for the reckless behavior.

But as Pepper turned toward her, the anger died on Blue's lips. Even in the dim light, she could see Pepper's swollen, tear-stained face and disheveled appearance. Something was very wrong.

Instantly switching gears, Blue jumped up and engulfed her sister in a tight hug. Pepper clung to her, fresh tears soaking into Blue's shirt. Gently stroking her messy hair, Blue asked, "Sweetie, what happened to you?"

Pepper pulled back, wiping her eyes roughly. When she spoke, her voice was choked with pain and bitterness. "He wasn't worth it after all."

Blue stiffened, alarm bells going off at her sister's implications combined with her obvious distress. Grasping Pepper's shoulders, she searched her face intently. "Did that boy try to hurt you?" she demanded.

Lip quivering, Pepper gave a small nod, fresh tears spilling down her cheeks. "When I told him to stop, he got really angry. Said I was teasing him and...and it wasn't fair." She inhaled shakily. "He kicked me out of his car and left me stranded miles from home. I've been walking for hours."

Red-hot fury coursed through Blue's veins even as her heart broke for her sister. She pulled Pepper close again, rubbing her back soothingly as the girl broke down sobbing.

"Shh, you're safe now. I've got you," Blue murmured. After several long minutes, Pepper's tears slowed. Blue gently wiped the moisture from her cheeks.

"What you did was reckless," she admonished quietly. "But you can always call me, no matter what. I will always come for you, Pepper. Always."

Sniffling, Pepper nodded remorsefully. "I know, I was just scared you'd be so disappointed in me." Fresh tears shimmered in her eyes.

"Never," Blue insisted firmly. "Your safety is all that matters to me. But that boy needs to face consequences."

Her voice hardened. "What's his name, Pepper?" When her sister hesitated, Blue grasped her shoulders imploringly. "Please. He can't be allowed to keep hurting girls like this."

Finally Pepper whispered a name, so softly it was nearly inaudible. But Blue heard it clearly. The boy who had dared lay a hand on her sister in violence. Rage simmered in her blood, but she kept her expression neutral.

227

"Get some rest," Blue instructed her gently. Retrieving a blanket, she tucked Pepper in snugly, then crossed to flick off the overhead light. At the door, she paused and looked back.

"Where are you going?" Pepper asked anxiously, sitting up in bed. The room was now dim, dawn's light filtering through the curtains.

Turning back, Blue gave her a reassuring smile. "Just stay here and sleep. You're safe now, I promise." She hoped her voice didn't betray the fury churning within.

Pepper still looked uncertain, so Blue walked back and gently stroked her hair. "Being a witch means nothing if I can't use magic to deal with nasty little punks who think they can hurt young girls," she said, steel underlying her soft tone.

Understanding dawned in Pepper's eyes, quickly followed by apprehension. "Just be careful," she implored quietly. "I don't want you getting in trouble because of me."

Blue squeezed her hand. "I'm always careful." Placing a kiss on her forehead, she again turned to leave. Glancing back once more from the doorway, she gave a playful wink. "Get some rest. I'll be back before you know it."

With that, she quietly descended the stairs and exited the house, wrath fueling each step. The first crimson rays of dawn glowed over the horizon as she climbed into her car. Soon the object of her fury would learn actions had consequences. The lesson was past due.

Starting the engine, Blue pulled smoothly away down the hushed street. She kept her focus straight ahead on the road, lest her churning emotions manifest tangibly. The town remained sleeping, unaware of the predator in their midst. But she would make certain he hurt no one else.

The drive passed in a blur, strategy and righteous fury warring within Blue's mind. Soon, the nondescript house appeared. It looked deceptively tranquil in the soft dawn light. But she knew evil lurked inside.

Well, not for much longer, Blue vowed. Magic could be wielded to protect just as easily as harm. Drawing a deep breath, she stepped from the car and strode up the walkway, fingers tingling with anticipation.

She rapped sharply on the front door three times. The sound seemed to linger in the heavy morning air. After an interminable wait, footsteps approached, and the door swung inward to reveal the scowling teenage boy, clad only in a wrinkled t-shirt and boxers.

Before he could react, Blue lunged forward, splaying her hand against his chest. "You will never touch another girl without her consent again," she hissed, magic flowing with the command.

The boy's eyes widened, mouth opening soundlessly. But Blue was already turning away, the cursed necklace in her palm growing warm as the spell took hold. She slipped it into her pocket safely.

The early birds were beginning to chirp as Blue descended the steps back to her car. The sun crested the horizon, spilling golden light over the neighborhood. Back in the boy's room, she knew he would be sinking into oblivious slumber, unaware of the critical lesson she had woven into his psyche.

Starting the engine, Blue began the drive back home, residual anger slowly dissipating with each mile. She had done what was necessary to protect others. Pepper would be safe now, as would any other girl who crossed that boy's path.

Pulling into the driveway just as the town was waking, Blue stretched her fingers, tingling fading. Inside, she could hear Pepper bustling around the kitchen, likely cooking up a big breakfast.

Smiling to herself, Blue exited the car and headed up the walkway. She pulled the necklace out of her pocket and clasped it around her neck. If that boy stepped out of line, the curse would cause him pain, and she would know.

She touched the necklace delicately and thought of another. One hidden in the back of her closet. While she no longer wore that one around her neck, its curse was no less potent.

Because Pepper had complained for a long time that Blue denied their powers, but what she didn't know was that Blue was capable of dark and terrible things.

Their father had learned that the hard way.

Thank you for reading!

© Sara Bourgeois 2023

Made in the USA
Monee, IL
12 October 2024

67801274R00128